Chapter One

It was magnificent. It had that feel right away. *Not just a house*, but a home. It was alive with regal character and grand essence. None of the things Julianne had listed under 'dream home' but this place was more than she had allowed herself to imagine.

It had been built in 1865, commissioned by the architect who had, along with another man designed most of St. Joseph. At that time the small Missouri town was just a few blocks long in any one direction, with the streets being named after the children of Joseph Robidoux, the man who founded the town in 1843.

It was a green, hilly paradise that made hard working traders and cattlemen into millionaires, in a day and age when a million dollars were more than any one person could spend. Though looking at the ornate stained glass windows and the grand detail that was put into this house, it would seem to Julianne that the architect had certainly tried.

She could only imagine, with such exquisite design outside, what would be waiting for them on the inside. She and Nick were a few minutes early for their meeting with the Realtor, and they were currently sitting in the long gravel driveway gaping at it through the windows of their silver Grand Cherokee. It was warm for a March day and they had the windows rolled down.

"My God." Her tone was one of whispery awe. "Just look at those windows. I never dreamt of owning a home like this. Are you sure it was listed within our budget?"

Nick smiled at his cautious wife. "Funny, I asked the Realtor the same thing. Apparently it was a foreclosure and has been empty for years. The bank is looking to unload it."

"Oh Nick! I love it"

"I know you do." He said smiling.

"Oh yeah? How do you know?" She asked, her tone slightly teasing.

"It's the way you bite your lip when you want something. And the sparkle in your eyes."

Julianne laughed at his description. "Just look at the back yard and the trees!"

"Yeah, well... Let's just hope that the interior restoration will be within our budget too..."

Julianne smiled at him knowingly. He was being cautious but she could feel it, this was their future home. She couldn't quite explain it, even to herself. She felt drawn to the house for reasons other than the beautiful windows and enormous yard. It was as if the house spoke to her. She couldn't wait to get inside.

They didn't have to wait long for the Realtor to arrive. Her name was 'Sherry spelled like Cherry' she'd informed him on the phone.

At first, Nick was a little concerned that "Cherry Sherry" was a little too bumpkin to find them the kind of place they were looking for. He was Bronx, born and bred and so far, everyone they had met in Missouri seemed a little bit hayseed. But now, looking at this place, he may have been a little quick to judge.

Cherry began gushing as soon as they hit the driveway. "Hello folks! Aren't you just the cutest little thing, and so pregnant! My goodness, you must be giving birth to a football player with the size of that belly!" Cherry laughed at her own joke.

"Actually twins." Julianne said with a genuine smile. She felt like there were two football players in there and they were beginning to scrimmage. They could feel mommy's excitement and were tumbling around.

"Oh my gosh! Twins! You are so blessed! Whose side of the family has twins?"

"Uh... that would be me." Nick raised his hand, hoping that Cherry would realize he had moved several feet closer to the front door. She did not.

"Uh oh. That means you have to kiss some serious mommy booty then! That barn she's hauling around is your fault!"

Cherry once again began to laugh. Julianne joined in, amused more by the lyrical sound of the woman's laughter than by the joke. She didn't really like being reminded that she was enormous.

Nick found himself laughing despite himself, more at her audacity than anything. However, Julianne seemed to be enjoying the woman, so he decided to keep the scoffing commentary on Cherry's ample weight to himself.

"Well I bet you folks are anxious to see the inside. The exterior does make for a grand first impression don't ya think?"

"Indeed." Nick replied, relieved to be moving at last.

Cherry immediately began driveling on about the history and the design of the house.

"Frederick Smith commissioned the house in 1865 to be built for his daughter and presented to her on her wedding day. Little did she know that her father and new husband had conspired to include secret rooms and hidden passages. It was rumored that the house was used as safe passage for Rebel Soldiers hiding from the Union forces.

Nick found the history interesting but immediately lost track of the conversation as soon as he laid eyes on the great hall inside.

They had come through two sets of ornately carved wood paneled doors, into a foyer where they both marveled at the sight of the gloriously wide grand staircase that curved in a graceful U shape up to the second floor. A hand-made banister with vine covered spindles placed a few inches apart, glided all the way up and around.

They could see a landing from the bottom of the stairs. It was large enough to set a couple of wing back chairs facing and enormous plate glass window that stretched nearly floor to ceiling.

The main level had 15-foot ceilings, with 11-foot doorways and the sides of the hall were lined with oak panels. The plaster walls were a foot thick between each room.

The first room off to the right, directly across from the foot of the grand stairs, was the sitting room. There were eight windows total and a stunning floor to ceiling mantelpiece that surrounded a large stone fireplace.

He could picture two antique chairs there, in the warm morning light that would enter the eastern side of the house. He could imagine placing a huge fragrant Christmas Tree in front of them during the holidays. A perfect picture.

On the north wall a doorway led into a large library. The magnificently paneled doors were open and Nick and Julianne both were excited to see thick dusty shelves full of old volumes.

"Do the books stay in the house?" Nick asked, incredulously. He couldn't believe that anyone would have abandoned such an incredible treasure.

"Oh yes. Many of the volumes belonged to the original owner of the house. The house passed down in the family and the books were passed along with it. The last owner passed away, leaving an unpaid mortgage and no heirs. So when they came in to auction the goods, they apparently chose to leave the books. Whomever decides to purchase the house will inherit an amazing collection."

Both he and Jules loved to read. He knew they would spend countless hours in that room with its bright lighting and seemingly endless shelves. They had always dreamt of owning an antique book collection, never really knowing how to begin. For Nick, it was a big point in favor of the house.

They chose to take a path through the gallery kitchen, which still had a huge wooden table residing in it. Then they traveled up the back stairs and down the wide upper hall. At the nearest end of the long hall was the only full bathroom in the house. Lined up along the eastern side were wood framed doorways, each leading to one of the three smaller bedrooms.

The master suite, at the far north east corner, consisted of a large bedroom, walk in closet, dressing area and half bath. There was also a door that led into the nursery. It was large and snuggled conveniently in the top of the turret just off the master bedroom. It was lined with evenly spaced windows around the octagon room, each with its own amazing view.

Opposite the bathroom, on the other end of the long hall, just around a slight corner, was the primary entrance to the nursery, a room that turned out to be a huge selling point for Julianne. This house had more than potential. They both loved what they were seeing and could picture raising their children here.

Perhaps that was why Nick decided not to tell her about the history of the house. *Well, that and the largest damn back yard I could ever hope to mow*, he thought

After the tour, they sat down with at the long wooden table in the kitchen with Cherry and began discussing the details.

"Why has this house been empty so long?" Julianne asked, trying hard but failing to keep the suspicion out of her voice.

"The location mostly. We discussed the neighborhood. Large minority population and higher petty crime area for St. Joe."

Nick ignored the implied racism in her comment. "Is there a lot of violent crime in St. Joe? You know, more than just the petty stuff?"

"Oh no! We rarely have anything of that sort. Mostly we get things like vandalism or home invasions while people are out. You get the occasional armed robbery but the last owner installed a good security system and never had any trouble. This is just an older part of town with low rent and property values."

"If we can manage a good night's sleep in the Bronx, we can surely get along fine in this neighborhood. We drove around before we came here. It didn't look so bad. It's a little old but there is quite a bit of renovation going on." Julianne commented.

"Oh yes. The city is focusing on revitalizing the entire 'Museum Hill' area. There are grants available for refurbishing. You would qualify if you chose to. There are restrictions of course if you go that route. Things have to be restored to their original condition." Cherry said.

"Hmmm." Nick hummed in reply, looking at his wife, a bit of excitement twirling in his belly. "Well, Jules?"

Julianne looked at Nick and then Cherry. "Do you mind if we take a few minutes to discuss it?" She asked the Realtor, who was practically drooling at the thought of selling the old mansion.

"I will leave the two of you. I will grab some paper work from my car and we can at least get the process started if you want to make an offer." She smiled.

"Do you think there are many offers on the place? You said it has been empty." Nick asked.

"No. I know for a fact that there are no other offers on this house. I also know that the bank refused to let it go for less than the list price, so if you want it you have to offer the full amount."

"Understood." Nick gave her a tight smile.

Cherry smiled again and hurried out the carport door.

Julianne looked at Nick and cautiously said "Well?" She was trying to keep the excitement at bay.

"From what I see, any renovations we would need to do would be within our budget. The electrical has been updated and the roof looks fairly new. We could offer list price and still be getting a steal. What do you think?"

Julianne's amazing smile let him know she wanted to buy it. "We can really afford it?"

"Let's ask to see the attic and the basement. If there isn't any major damage to either, then I think we should take it." He said.

Julianne squealed as she wiggled her way up from the table and headed toward the door. Cherry was out in the drive talking on the phone, probably to the bankers.

"We are heading up to check out the attic." Julianne called to her. Cherry nodded and turned back to her phone call.

Julianne wondered for a moment what they would find up there. She noticed that Cherry's face had taken on a bit of a pinched-look and she was talking quietly and quickly in to the phone. Deciding it might not have anything to do with the house, she went back in and joined her husband at the foot of the kitchen stairs.

"Shall we go up?" She asked.

"We? No. Me? Yes. The floor might not be sturdy or there could be water damage. It's safer if you wait for me here. I will only take a quick look."

"Party-pooper." She said and headed to sit back down at the kitchen table.

True to his word, Nick was back within ten minutes having checked both attic and basement.

"How bad is it?"

"Surprisingly good. Not a lot of ventilation up stairs but like Cherry said, I could install an attic fan to help air it out. The basement was dark but I could see that it was in good shape, no cracks in the walls or obvious water damage. We will have to have it inspected of course but... I think we are good to go." He smiled at his wife as he dusted his hands across his jeans.

"You really think so?" Julianne asked excitedly.

"Well, you know I am just an architect what do I know?" They both laughed. He knew a lot.

Nick walked to the kitchen door and hollered out to Cherry.

"Hey lady, you just sold yourself a house!"

The tension left Cherry's face and she did a little victory dance in the driveway. "You two are gonna love it here!"

Chapter Two

Her first morning in the house, Julianne woke to the smell of breakfast. The delicious aroma of biscuits and bacon mingled perfectly with the strong smell of coffee. She smiled to herself. Her husband had grown quite adorable since he found out that she was pregnant. She felt so lucky to have a man who treated her so well and so looked forward to starting a family with her.

She propped herself up on one arm and looked at the clock. It was 6 o'clock in the morning! A tad bit early for Nick to be cooking. Just as she was pushing the covers off, a rustling sound in near proximity had her pulse jumping into her throat. She sat up quickly and looked behind her. The sleeping lump of her husband was shifting into a more comfortable position. *Well then, who is cooking*, she wondered?

She pulled the covers the rest of the way off her legs, careful not to lift them too high and let cold air in on Nick. She slid off the edge of the tall four-post bed and slipped her chilly feet into her warm and fuzzy house shoes. She rose slowly, trying not to wake him, and quickly grabbed her robe off the post and wrapped herself in its warmth. She gave the dogs a quick scratch behind their ears and signaled for them to stay put as she crossed the room to the door.

It swung open easily, without sound. It gave her a warm feeling. Nick had told her that a quiet door was a sign of a sturdy home. She loved their new home. She had a comfortable feeling of belonging here. She couldn't quite explain it but it felt something like pleasant de ja'-vu.

She made her way down the long hall to the kitchen stairs. She patted silently down, taking in the aroma, feeling her stomach begin to growl as she approached the source. She half expected to find her best friend or her mom slaving away at the oven, not stopping to consider how they would have gotten in, or why they would have driven from Kansas City so early.

She could hear the telltale sounds of mixing bowls and saucers clanking. A soft female voice spoke but she couldn't understand what it said. Another, equally soft but more masculine voice replied in a harsh whisper and then the kitchen fell silent.

As she got to the bottom, Julianne peaked around the doorframe at the stove. It should have been red with heat and the kitchen should have been alive with activity but it wasn't. Frowning, Julianne stepped into the kitchen and looked around. The room was empty. Nothing stirred except a few particles of dust that were dancing around in the sun light that filtered in through the lace curtains.

"I don't understand," she said aloud.

As she stood there looking around, the wonderful scents that had aroused her from sleep were fading quickly away. She blinked in confusion and then started to giggle.

"I must have been dreaming. Is that your way of letting me know that you're hungry little ones?" She asked her pooch of a belly. She hadn't decided on names yet, they weren't sure of the sex of the children. She had secretly been wishing for a couple of identical girls.

She took it as a good sign that the nursery was done in soft shades of vanilla and pink. It had well-drawn, soft looking velveteen rabbits lounging in various poses all over the walls. A thick, soft, maroon velvet border ran around at waist height, separating the smoky pink and vanilla shades of the rabbits from a soft mauve wall below. It was a large nursery, plenty of room for two of everything. It was perfect for a couple of girls.

Julianne caressed her belly, day dreaming as she studied the contents of the refrigerator. Suddenly she was ravenous. She began digging around in the new fridge for something that appealed to the babies' appetites. The episode with the breakfast dream was completely forgotten.

Spying a carton of farm fresh eggs and a drawer full of veggies, she began pulling out ingredients: Onion, garlic, celery, green peppers, cheese and bacon. The baby really seemed to like bacon.

She warmed up two iron skillets, one for the bacon and the other for an omelet. It wasn't long after she began sizzling the bacon in the skillet, that she could hear the rattle of dog tags and the sleepy footsteps of her husband coming down the kitchen stairs.

"Good morning." She smiled at Nick's rumpled hair and tired expression.

"Hmmm..." he grinned at her as he poured a mug of coffee. "How did you sleep?"

"Like a log. The babies too. Hope that is a sign that they will both sleep through the night once they're born."

"We can dream," he said as he wrapped his arms around her from behind.

He cradled her tummy as though he couldn't wait to hold their children. He was as excited about being a dad as any man she had ever seen. He was already tossing out names.

"What about Liam for a boy?" She asked him while stirring the eggs.

"Good Irish name." He replied, stealing a bite of cheese over her shoulder.

"Yes. That would make your parents very happy."

"Indeed." He smiled. His folks were very proud of their Irish heritage. As were hers of her Portuguese background.

"What about Ana Silva for a girl?" He suggested, incorporating her maiden name as a middle name in true Portuguese tradition.

"Ugh. No, not Silva. I kinda like Ana though with the Portuguese spelling."

"We still have plenty of time to find just the right name."

They finished preparing breakfast, enjoyed a lazy meal over the newspaper and then cleaned up the dishes together before heading back up to the bedroom. The only working bathroom in the house was at the end of the long hall upstairs. It was the only complaint Julianne had about the house.

There was a second bathroom under the grand staircase downstairs but from the look of the browned porcelain stool, it had been out of service for quiet a while. There was a half bath off the master bedroom but Nick was in the process of tearing it out.

Nick promised that as soon as they were finished unpacking the bedroom, he would begin renovating the house in earnest. He would knock out a wall between the master and second bedroom and design a huge bathroom with plenty of room for all her soaps, lotions and perfumes.

He was a great husband. Julianne could not believe how wonderful her life had become over the past two years. She had been in such a bad place when she first met Nick. Her first husband had been dead for almost a year but she hadn't managed to put it behind her yet.

Meeting Nick at the cancer awareness run had changed her life. He had lost his sister to cancer and had come to a place of wisdom one only gets with experience and time. He had helped her learn to focus on Jeremy's life rather than his death and convinced her the best way to honor his memory was to do the one thing he could no longer do.

Live. Really live. Be in the moment and have gratitude for all that was good in her life. It wasn't long after that she started feeling more than friendship for Nick and not very long after that, he admitted the same. He had been so worried about taking advantage of her in her grief he had waited months to tell her how he felt.

Afterward, they had a bit of a whirlwind romance. Within three months they were living together and within six they were engaged. Opting for a simple small ceremony amongst the fall leaves at the City Park, they were married two months after he proposed.

Six months into the marriage she was pregnant. It was what they were both hoping for. It wasn't like they were young and impetuous. She was 35 and he was 38 the perfect age to have children in her opinion.

He had never married, instead spending the bulk of his bachelor-hood chasing his career as an architect. He had gotten rather well known in Chicago and had planned to stay there but his sister took ill and he found the importance of family out weighing the prestige of money. He had headed back to New York. He never regretted his decision to leave the windy city.

Julianne had married at 22 and was widowed at 33. They had gone into a fertility specialist after quite a few years trying to get pregnant. During routine blood work they discovered that her husband had late stage testicular cancer and had no remaining viable sperm. It was a terrible blow. They had gone in, discussing plans for a nursery and visions of several children and many grandchildren surrounding them in their old age.

They had come out knowing they were never going to be parents and Jeremy wasn't going to grow old. It was the death of her dreams. Shortly after, it was real death. It was like a giant cosmic slap in the face and it took a year for Julianne's grief to abate enough to move his watch from the tray on her dresser.

Nick felt humbled that a woman who loved as deeply as Julianne chose to love him. He watched her forge ahead and burn through the terrible grief and make a life for herself again. If she could know how amazing she looked through his eyes, she would never feel insecure.

It wasn't just about her beauty, he thought her as near to perfect as she could be. 5'10" with long graceful legs she looked him square in the eye. She wasn't overly thin, and she had great curves. Her long chestnut hair curled gently around her oval face. Her full mouth was quick to flash a pearly white smile that reached the depth of her large hazel eyes.

He was, in his own opinion, a little bit on the skinny side. He had always been told that his crystal blue eyes, thick long black lashes and shaggy brown-blonde hair gave him a mysterious bad boy image, but he never bought into it. He had lived a perfectly 'Leave-it-to-Beaver' life, and had never done anything more dangerous than the occasional, leisurely motorcycle ride on a sunny afternoon.

She was the type of woman who was completely capable of taking care of herself but still loved to be cared for once in a while. She was so much wiser than he was and probably the smartest person he had ever met. She was really good at being married and guided him along. He never doubted her love for him. She made sure he felt it every day.

He wasn't going to do anything to spoil her dream of a great house, happy dogs and a couple of smiling kiddies running in the halls.

With this in mind, Nick waited until she was in the shower, and then booted up the laptop and opened his Punch Pro program. He opened the design he had been working on. He wanted to create the ultimate bathroom. It had to be the right room for mommy and her new babies, a room with the perfect balance of practicality and luxury.

He was well into the tile design for behind the large tub, where he planned a lush atrium, when he felt his wife's wet locks slide against his shirtless back. He hit the save icon and quickly slammed the laptop shut. He moved the computer to the floor and turned to sweep his wife up and dump her in a fit of laughter onto the bed. He straddled her robed figure and poked his finger playfully into her face.

"I said no peaking!"

Her child like laughter prevented her from being able to answer her husband's charges. She wound her long graceful arms around his neck and pulled him in for a kiss. In seconds, his blood was boiling and he found himself slipping the robe open around her luscious breasts.

"Don't! I am as fat as a cow!" She howled.

"Maybe a pot bellied pig," he chided, "but look at these babies!" He grabbed a handful of breast and massaged it gently.

She moaned a quick response. He slipped open her robe and made love to her in the bright morning light. It was always the same, tender and gentle at the start and pure heat at the end.

When they had sated their desire, they stayed in bed, discussing their plans for the house. It was a lazy Sunday morning and they had nothing to do besides plan the renovations and explore their beautiful new home. When they were ready to begin their exploration, they started for the attic, deciding to start at the top and work their way down. Even at the end of March, by the afternoon the attic would be a sweltering space of heat and humidity. It was better to get it out of the way in the morning.

They made their way up the dusty dimly lit stairs. They curved up and to the left in a wide arc. By the time they reached the top, they could smell the musty aroma that lingered there. They wanted to install an attic fan to help get rid of it.

They were both examining the rafters when they heard a loud series of thuds from downstairs. They both went instantly still. Slowly, they turned and looked at one another.

"What was that?" Julianne said with a modicum of apprehension to her tone. Her jaw tense, her eyes wide she looked to her husband for an explanation.

"It sounded like it came from downstairs. Let's see, what would be right below us?"

"Well we came up and to the left and went right at the top of the stairs, so the master staircase?"

"I hope no one fell down the stairs. Who would be here?"

"Surely not," she said turning to head back down to the second floor, forgetting her discomfort for a moment.

"The dogs would have alerted if some one was in the house, maybe a piece of the banister fell off or something," Nick suggested as he followed her toward the attic staircase.

Chapter Three

Julianne neared the bottom of the attic stairs when Nick reached his hand forward intending to slow her down so that he could pass in front of her. He wanted to be the first one to come around the corner at the bottom, just in case they did have an intruder. As his fingers brushed her elbow, she shrieked and flailed backwards. Nick grabbed her, unsure of what was happening, thinking perhaps he had startled her.

As he pulled her close to him, he could see that the bottom three stairs had basically disintegrated under his wife's feet, and were now clanking loudly down into the bedroom closet below. If he hadn't already been reaching for her, Julianne could very well have toppled after them.

They stood still for a moment, holding each other tightly, eyes glued to the hole in the stairs. Julianne leaned against him, a dry sob escaping her throat. She looked at him, her hand protectively fluttering over her abdomen. She didn't have to tell him what she was thinking. He knew, she was thinking about the babies.

The fear that welled up inside of him had him barking at Julianne to stay put. She merely nodded and watched as Nick jumped the gap. Another sob escaped her as he landed on the other side of the four-foot hole.

"It's alright. I made it easy. Now listen to me Jules. I am going to brace my foot against the step there that you are standing on. Now I don't know how solid it is so you are going to have to jump a little bit okay?"

"Jump?" She asked, clearly unnerved. "I'm seven months pregnant with twins Nick! How am I supposed to jump?" She was shaking her head rapidly, panic rising in her voice.

"Don't worry, I am going to grab you as soon as you are in the air babe. I will make sure you land upright, okay?"

"Nick, I don't know about this."

"Trust me. Besides, what other options do we have? You can't stay up there and there isn't any other way down."

"Ooooh!" It was a fearful half moan, half cry and it nearly broke Nick's heart.

"Oh, babe. It will be all right. Have I ever let you down?"

"No. Okay... crap! What do you want me to do?"

"Just grab my hand and try to hop over the hole onto the landing next to me okay? I will pull you over and catch you as you land. I promise."

Jules took a deep breath, and putting her faith in Nick she hopped. As soon as her back foot left the stair, she felt herself being pulled forward into Nick. They collided, but Nick kept them both on their feet. He pulled her into a tight hug, then he jerked her back so he could look her over.

"Are you alright?" He asked, still holding tightly to her upper arms.

She nodded, the tears welling in her eyes and the sob caught in her throat prevented her from speaking. She rubbed his elbows. He eased his grip but kept a hand under her elbow as they headed back down the long hall toward the front staircase. For a moment they had both forgotten the noise they had heard.

Then, as they got closer to the bedroom where Nick intended to put her in bed, they could hear a shuffling noise coming from the foyer on the first floor. They both stopped in their tracks, frozen for a moment in surprise and uncertainty.

"Hello?" Nick asked, protectively moving in front of his wife. He was feeling the electricity build. He could feel the cold tendrils of fear circling his ribs and sliding up the back of his neck.

No one answered his call. He and Julianne moved quickly to the top of the stairs and looked down over the railing. They could see the area rug that was placed at the bottom of the stairs. They could not see anything else.

"Hello?" Nick said again.

When again no one answered Nick motioned for Julianne to let the dogs out of the bedroom and stepped down a couple of steps to gain a larger view.

As soon as Julianne opened the door, the dogs bolted from the bedroom. They shot straight down the stairs passed Nick, giving no heed to his signals to heal or stay. They got to the bottom and skidded across the rug and into the formal living room. As soon as they were around the corner, they began barking and snarling in the back corner of the room.

Nick followed them down quickly, pretending that he was not afraid for his wife's sake. Julianne followed as far as the landing half way down and watched as Nick moved quickly into the room. The dogs continued to bark for a moment, before obeying Nick's command for silence. Then nothing.

A few seconds passed and Julianne took a few timid steps down. As she became level with the living room, she caught site of herself in the old oval mirror on top of the mantelpiece on the opposite wall. It startled her; she didn't recognize herself for a moment. Then she realized there was another reflection in the mirror as well. There was someone standing behind her on the landing.

She whirled around, grabbing the banister to steady her self, calling out for Nick at the same time. Her heart beat against her rib cage and the air was scraping in and out of her aching lungs. A chill ran down her back and her hand gripped the railing so hard her knuckles went white.

"It's okay. There's no one here." He said as he came back through the doorway.

Julianne spun back around, never letting go of the banister and looked wildly at Nick and then back at the landing.

As soon as he saw his wife's face, he knew something was wrong. He loped up the stairs two at a time and was at her side in a split second. He grabbed her by the shoulders, spinning her to face him.

"What is it?"

The look of concern on Nick's face made her feel foolish. She smiled and shook her head, extending one hand out to his face to caress his jaw in a familiar way. Trying to look repentant.

"Nothing. I'm sorry! I'm fine. I just thought I saw something..." her sentence trailed off as she looked back at the mirror and again over her shoulder.

"It must have been a reflection. I was already feeling creeped out by the dogs and just let my imagination get away from me.

Hoping to distract him from the reprimand she could see forming on his lips, she asked, "What were the dogs after?"

"I don't know." He said whistling for the dogs to join them. "They were just staring at the corner above the window."

"At the ceiling?" Julianne asked confused.

"Yeah. Right at the corner, behind the wing back chair."

"Well, what could that be all about?"

"I don't know. Maybe they heard a squirrel or mouse in the wall. I'll call pest control tomorrow and have them take a look. I think we need to have the place checked for termites too. Something ate the crap out of those steps up there."

"What is that?" Julianne said, not hearing what her husband was saying.

At first, Nick didn't see what she was referring to. He looked up at her, the question on his face and she pointed to a spot near the edge of the area rug. With a second look, he spotted a silvery but not quite shiny object lying on the floor.

He went back down the stairs and picked it up. He turned it over in his hand and looked closely at it before turning it over to Julianne who had followed him down.

"It's an old clasp, the kind gentleman used to pin their scarves to their neck. My granddad has one that belonged to his pop. What's it say on the back?"

She raised it up close to her face and read the series of small letters engraved in the back. "H. W. S." She said handing it back to Nick.

He looked closely at it, rubbing his thumb over the surface once. He looked back at Jules, an ornery grin on his face. "Kinda girlie writing. Think this guy must be a little light in his loafers."

Julianne shook her head. He was attempting to lighten the mood so she let the crass remark go unnoticed. She couldn't help but correct him though. "Not girlie Nick, *old.*"

"Well, I wonder how that got there." He murmured looking up at the ceiling, as if perhaps it fell from somewhere, jarred loose when the stairs crashed down on the floor above. He didn't wonder long.

"Hmm. Well, I have to get my tools out and get a board nailed over that opening in the attic stairs until I can get a couple of guys out here to shore it up. In the meantime, my lovely but pregnant wife, I don't want you to try to go up there."

"Oh, no worries. I have no intention of climbing those stairs again any time soon. It stinks up there and motherhood has gifted me with a bionic nose."

He handed her the little metal clasp and headed toward the kitchen. Not wanting to be alone at that particular moment, she slipped the clasp in her pocket and trailed after him.

"What do you think you are doing?" He asked her in a playful tone.

"I'm gonna help!" she said in a voice reserved for small children and women who are trying to be cute.

"Okay, but I do all the heavy lifting." He patted her bottom as she passed in front of him into the kitchen.

They spent a good hour getting the plywood and tools up the stairs, and across the hole. It looked a little bit like a wheelchair ramp and it made the formerly scary attic stairs seem a little more mundane. Jules felt sillier than ever about her fright in the mirror. She decided to pass it off as nerves and forget the matter completely.

After they were finished putting the tools back in their boxes, they decided to have a quick lunch. Normally they would have gone for cold cuts and maybe a potato salad, but the twins had a different idea. They wanted fried food.

Julianne had never liked fried food before and found it very disconcerting that the whims of her unborn children could so easily over ride her own. Nick of course found it amusing.

So instead of a light, well-balanced meal, they had grilled cheese and French- fries. Total carbs and fat. Julianne just knew it was all going to go to her butt. Nick found this funny as well. In his eyes, she was perfect. If her butt got bigger, it was just more of her to love.

After lunch they decided to explore the rooms and closets on the second floor. They were hoping for a forgotten antique, a box of old love letters or some other incredible old treasure.

At first their search yielded little more than cobwebs and dust bunnies. They were heading into their last bedroom feeling disappointed.

"Damn. I was really hoping to find something. Maybe an old dress or a pair of ladies shoes." Julianne said.

"Oh, I dunno... I think I would rather have found an old textile, something worth a billion bucks." Nick said turning the knob on the closet door.

"Nick look!" Julianne said with excitement as he swung the door open.

Inside the closet was an old toy box. It was a fairly simple design and not very big. It was made up of sanded and painted 2x4s. The wear and tear on the paint suggested immediately that it was old. The wheels were iron, and they made a terrible moan when Nick wheeled it into the bedroom for closer inspection.

The only ornamentation on the box was a paint job. It was scratched but you could still see the faded horses with their faded cowboys tilting their hats as they rode off into the sunset. It had little rope handles on both sides, and a latch that was in the shape of a cowboy boot on the front. The latch met up with a dull edged spur locking the lid in place.

"Well, I doubt it's worth a billion dollars, but I guess I could fix it up a bit and put it in the babies room. I'll have to take the spur off and sand it down pretty good before I paint it yellow."

"Ugh. Not yellow."

"Well we can't very well do pink. We might end up with a boy."

"So? Even if both were boys, what's wrong with having a pink room?" Julianne was just goading him and could barely conceal her smile.

"No way! We'd end up with sissies!"

"Oh Nick!" Julianne said laughing, "pink doesn't make a boy a sissy. Or gay."

"Maybe it does or maybe it doesn't. Either way, if we have boys, those velveteen rabbits are goners."

Julianne laughed at Nick again. He was far from perfect but she loved him anyway.

Nick bent down and lifted the lid. "It's empty."

Julianne shrugged. "Sounds like the wheels could use a little grease."

Nick nodded his agreement. "Let's see what else we can find, we'll move it to the nursery later." He wheeled it back into the closet.

They held hands as they continued through out the rest of the upstairs. There were linen closets that lined the entire length of the hallway. They were empty, as were the cabinets in the bathroom.

They did not find any more antique treasures, but did discover that one of the bedrooms had a wonderful mural of a sad fairy painted on the back of the door. The tear that fell from one eye almost looked as though it was actually made of liquid. They both marveled at the creativity and wondered aloud how the artist had made the tear drop sparkle the way water does when it catches the sun.

They decided to head back down the grand staircase and check out the multitude of antique volumes they knew were waiting for them in the library. Julianne remembered seeing several Charles Dickens novels that looked as though they might have been first editions.

She found a copy of Bleak House and pulled it from the shelves.

"Did you know that Charles Dickens was ripped off by American printers? There weren't any international copyright agreements at that time. Certain publishers gave him royalties but many did not. He wasn't the only one, there were many British authors whose works were pirated."

"Really? That's terrible! I wonder if the copy you are holding was one of those infringed copies."

"Whoa! I hadn't thought of that! Let me see who published this copy." She flipped open the first page and read that 'Harper Brother's' had printed that copy.

"Hmm. I am not sure if they were one of the honorable exceptions or not. I will have to look it up later." She said, sliding the book back into its spot. She stepped sideways as she read additional titles.

As they were searching through the shelves, Nick came across a large book of maps. They were folded copies of hand drawn maps dating back into the middle of the nineteenth century. Each was preserved in its own plastic pocket.

"Jules! Take a look at this! It's incredible. It is a hand drawn map of St. Joe!" He unfolded the map and laid it out on his desk. It was very large, six feet high by nine feet wide, he estimated. He grabbed a magnifying glass from the cardboard box that was marked "office."

"Oh man! Look at that detail." She replied looking over his shoulder at the map.

"Yeah, the artist was outstanding. I don't see his name but the map is called Bird's Eye View, St. Joseph 1863."

"The scale is just amazing! Such tiny little houses."

"Here, look through this." He said handing her the magnifying glass.

"Oh wow... hey look there is Messanie Street.... And there is Sylvanie."

She traced her finger lightly up the old yellowing paper until she found what she was looking for.

"There! That would be us, or rather the land, it doesn't look like the house had been built yet. Though that small church must be Twin Spires."

"Correction, it is Immaculate Conception now but no... it wasn't built yet so that must be the church before it. The one that was burned down..."

"Oh yeah, that history book at the library mentioned something about that." She continued to run the glass over the map. She came back to the spot where their house had been built and she froze.

"What is that behind the church?" She asked Nick, handing the glass back to him.

"Where?" He said following the familiar streets to the point on the map to which she was referring.

"There." She said pointing. "Right where the apartment building next door sits now."

"Huh." Nick said sounding uneasy. "I'm not sure but they seem to look like..."

"Crosses?" Jules said, finishing his sentence.

Nick put the magnifying glass down for a minute. "It sure kinda looks like it."

"Look at the legend! That means headstones! Ew! That's kinda creepy." Jules squealed. Exaggerating the shiver that ran down her spine.

Nick laughed out loud. He folded up the bottom of the map and turned to face his wife. He sat on the edge of the desk and pulled her in for a hug. She kissed the top of his head and declared herself ready for a nap.

"Madam, your chariot awaits," he said scooping her up in to his arms.

She squealed and laughed with delight. Even as pregnant as she was, he still made her feel dainty. He carried her all the way up the grand staircase and into the master bedroom. He deposited her onto the bed between the giant slumbering dogs.

"I'll get you a glass of water." He said, kissing her forehead.

He left the room for a few seconds and came back with a glass, which he set on the night table closest to his wife. She was already breathing deeply, well on her way to sleep.

Nick decided to work on his design for the master bathroom. He grabbed his laptop, sat back against the headboard next to Julianne. He popped it open and signed on, fully expecting to see the design he'd been working on still open on the screen.

Instead his screen lit slowly to reveal a scrambled mess where his desktop should be. He fiddled for a while, trying to clear up the screen and retrieve his blueprint. He had made a couple of really inspired design changes and didn't want to lose his work.

After trying to end task and revert back to last saved, he ended up having to shut it completely down and restart the computer. When the computer came back up, the screen once again looked normal. He clicked on his blueprint folder looking for the one he had saved as "The queen's lavatory." It was not there.

He opened his program and dropped the file menu. There at the bottom, queen's lavatory was listed. He double clicked it and was greeted with a sharp sound and an error box stating that the pathway was incorrect.

"Damn it!" He cursed lightly under his breath. He decided he would call Palmer, his tech support guy. Palmer worked at the store where Nick bought the lap top and was a real whiz. If anyone could save the file it would be him.

It was almost six in the evening on Sunday. Nick figured he could catch the kid at home but all he got was voice mail. He set the lap top gently on the desk and quietly stepped out into the hall and left a quick message explaining his dilemma.

He headed back into the room, rubbing the tension from his face. Deciding that he too could use a nap, he lowered himself gently onto the bed. Julianne snuggled into him without opening her eyes. He was feeling very warm and cozy, on the verge of nodding off when he felt his wife's breathing change.

Instead of the soft steady breathing of sleep, hers sounded raspy and shallow. The sudden change alarmed him.

He lifted his head slightly and whispered her name. She didn't respond. He raised up onto an elbow and peered over her shoulder. Her breathing was becoming more shallow and rapid. Her face was getting very pale.

"Jules?" He shook her lightly but she did not respond.

'Julianne!" He said more loudly as he shook her again.

Chapter Four

Julianne dreamt. She was alone in her bedroom and it was the middle of the night. She could see the alarm clock blinking 3:11 AM. She was confused as to why it was blinking and concerned about Nick, though she couldn't quite remember why.

She looked around the bedroom at the soft maple furniture that didn't belong to her. Her newly purchased four poster bed was now a large sloping sleigh bed with an unusual number of pillows on it. She lay ensconced in them, feeling as though she could not move. She wanted to get out of bed and look for Nick.

Before she could expend much effort trying to rise, a woman walked in through the door that adjoined the nursery to the master bedroom. She was carrying something in both arms but her image was fuzzy, like looking through a soft focus lens, or like someone had smeared Vaseline over her eyes.

She could sense that whatever the woman held was of extreme importance to her. She strained her eyes to get a better look. She couldn't really tell but it seemed to her that whatever it was, moved anxiously in the matronly woman's grasp.

"There, there now," the woman cooed in a voice thick with Irish brogue, " be still now. You don't be wanting me to drop you on your precious wee head now do ya? Can't you be still like your sister?"

Julianne still wasn't positive of what the women held but felt very anxious to find out. "Please, come closer." She said without forming the words.

"Oh, don't you worry now, I'll take the babes. You'll have plenty to do without them."

Julianne stared at the woman. She tried to focus on the details. She could make out swirling strands of gray hair that had escaped the confines of the woman's white bonnet. She could see the contrast of what appeared to be some sort of apron hanging over a long charcoal dress that did not quiet reach the floor but she could not see the woman's feet.

"You rest, you're going to need your strength to move out of here."

"Move out? We aren't moving out, we are moving in." Jules said confused by the woman's words.

"No dear, that is what your plan *was* but if you want to see your wee ones, you'll change that plan and move right back out."

The woman sounded almost as though she was singing. The contrast between the lulling voice and the menacing words confused Julianne even more.

"But I want to see the babies... Nick? Do you know where Nick is?" Julianne asked, again without forming words.

"He's just where you left him, don't you know where that is?" The woman answered sharply.

Julianne tried to shake her head but it seemed to be glued to the satiny pillow behind her. She wanted to sit up. She wanted to take the bundles from the woman's arms. The babes, the woman had said. Were there two? Where they hers?

She couldn't quite remember. *I must be dreaming*, she thought. Nick, she had to find Nick. Something was wrong. She tried again to say his name but her lips wouldn't move.

"Don't strain yourself lass, you'll find him. Say goodbye to the wee ones." The woman walked back through the nursery door, laughing.

"You don't have to worry about them anymore."

Just as she turned away with the babies, another woman appeared. She was beautiful with dark creamy skin and penetrating green eyes. But her face was twisted in anger and agony. Immediately Julianne began to panic.

"He took everything from me! Now I will take everything from him!" The raven-haired beauty screamed at Julianne.

In a split second the woman was over the bed and thrust her hand into Julianne's chest and began to squeeze.

The pain overwhelmed her. She could feel pressure building in her chest. The woman would not let go.

"He took my life, my chance at a family!"

"No!" Julianne screamed. "NICK!"

Chapter Five

Nick's heart was pounding loudly in his chest. He could hear his blood roaring through his ears. He felt panic bubble in his throat. In the far back reaches of his mind he wondered if he was having a heart attack. The entire front of his mind was focused on his wife, who was writhing in his arms, sweating and moaning in her sleep.

He said her name again, lightly shaking her, trying to get her to open her eyes. When she began to cry and called out 'NICK!' All gentility left him and he began shaking her in earnest.

"Julianne!" He said it loudly but to his ear it sounded thin and nearly a whisper.

He grabbed her around the waist and slid her upward until she was in a sitting position, with her back against the headboard. He put his head to her chest to listen for her heartbeat.

He could hear it, strong and rapid but it was accompanied by the harsh rasping wind that passed for his wife's breathing. He pulled quickly back from her and stared hard at her face as she began to gasp and cough and clutch her chest. She was awake, looking confused and searching the room as though she were looking for someone.

"Jules! Are you all right?

"Nick... where... what's happening?" Julianne sounded gruff and confused.

"I think you are sick baby. You're pale and wheezing. How do you feel?"

"Like my head is in a balloon. I had the strangest dream..." She barely got the words out before a wave of nausea dropped over her like a hot wet blanket. She lurched to her side and grabbed the trashcan next to the bed.

Recognizing the motion from the weeks of morning sickness, Nick caught her hair and held it out of the way as his wife vomited the undigested remains of her lunch. After two or three productive heaves, she began to gag and cough.

Nick traced light comforting circles on her back with the palm of his hand. He slipped an arm under her side and gently pulled her back into a sitting position.

"You okay?" He asked, handing her a glass of water that was sitting on the table next to the bed.

She started to answer but her lungs caught and she began coughing the air out, feeling the ache in her abdomen and diaphragm. She grabbed at her baby bump and moaned.

"That's it. We are going to the emergency room. Right now." He swung his legs over the side of the bed, pulling the covers down with him

"Nick!" she said, sipping at the water.

"Do not argue with me woman. We are going to the hospital. You are pregnant and obviously sick, and we are not taking any chances."

His tone was light but Julianne recognized the fear in his eyes. She also recognized his stubborn determination.

"Okay. I'll get up and get dressed," she said quietly.

"Nope. You are going to sit right there and I am going to bring you your clothes. Then I am going to carry you down the stairs and to the car. Don't argue." He said, wagging a finger at her.

Julianne smiled to herself. She liked the take charge side of her husband. She knew that underneath the strong facade, he was terrified and she loved him all the more for being brave anyway. Still, the rough exterior was alluring.

She did what Nick told her to do, waiting in bed as he pulled together an almost normal looking outfit. As she pushed herself to the edge of the bed, she realized how tired she was. She was glad they were going to the hospital.

Better to be safe than sorry, she thought. And from no where in particular the thought, *I hope I am not too late*, echoed in her brain.

Chapter Six

"What was the dream about?" Nick asked her as they sat in the sitting area, waiting for a nurse to call her name.

"Hmm?" She said, looking up from the magazine in her lap.

"When you woke up, you said you'd had the strangest dream. Do you remember what it was about?"

"No. I rarely do." She smiled, meeting her husbands worried gaze.

"I just thought we could try our hand at dream interpretation, see what has you so worried."

"That's easy! I am terrified of trying to squeeze two babies the size of a meatloaf through a passage way about as big as a hot dog!" Julianne said laughing until she coughed.

"Easy!" Nick patted her gently on the back. A nurse appeared through a door marked *Urgent Care*, and called Julianne's name. Nick helped her to her feet and kept a supportive arm around the small of her back as they made their way down a hall and into an exam room.

Nick helped Julianne get herself onto the end of the exam table. The nurse, whose name was Patricia, strapped the blood pressure cuff on her arm and slipped a thermometer into her mouth. Her blood pressure was a little bit on the low side but she was not running a fever. She breathed in and out on command, and the nurse listened through the frozen end of her stethoscope.

She made a few notations on the chart and left the room after saying the doctor would be right with them.

"Why do they always lie to you and tell you the doctor will be right with you? They are never right with you." Nick muttered.

"At least they have magazines in this one." Jules replied.

After fifteen minutes of flipping through Golf Digest, Nick was relieved to hear the doctor removing the chart and coming through the door.

After a brief introduction the doctor, a robust woman with silver hair and glasses that she kept dangling around her neck on a thick silver chain, read quickly over the notes in the chart.

"How far along are you misses Sullivan?"

"29 weeks," she said squirming uncomfortably on the end of the table.

"You experienced vomiting and you were light headed?"

"Yeah. I woke up feeling dizzy."

"Have you had much nausea since the first trimester?"

"No."

"Any chest pain or abdominal pain?"

"No."

"Any spotting?"

"No."

"Good." She took Julianne's wrist and briefly timed her pulse.

"Well my dear, I think you are the millionth patient to present symptoms of the flu today." She smiled at Julianne and scratched a few notes into her chart.

"You go home, take it easy and drink plenty of water. Double up on your pre-natals for the next two days and stay warm and dry. The biggest concern we have with the flu during pregnancy is the development of pneumonia. I will send a copy of your chart to your OB so she can give you a follow up at your next appointment."

With that, the matronly woman smiled sweetly at Nick and headed toward the door.

"Thank you Doctor." They said in unison as Nick helped Julianne off the table.

They stopped at drug store on the way home for 7-Up and saltines, something that had been a staple of Julianne's diet for the first few months of pregnancy.

"I feel as heavy as lead. I need to get into a warm tub."

Nick immediately objected to the idea. "She said stay dry Jules."

"I know honey, but she meant stay out of the rain. She didn't intend for me not to bathe for the next nine weeks!"

When they arrived back at the house, he deposited her once again into the master bedroom. He told her to stay put while he walked the dogs and he would draw her a bath when he returned.

She agreed, reluctant to be alone. "Just hurry," she told him.

"Back in a flash."

He gave signal to the dogs, and the three of them patted happily down the front stairs. Julianne sat alone, listening to the house. She was feeling uneasy. She felt like someone was watching her. Giving in to the fear a little bit, she pushed her back firmly against the headboard and pulled a pillow over her baby bump. She looked around the room. Nothing was out of place but she had the strong sense that something was not right.

As her gaze glided over to the nursery door, she had a flash of memory. She remembered seeing the woman standing in the doorway, holding the twins. A cold shock of fear filled her heart and she knew that the woman had said something important.

She strained to remember more, closing her eyes and trying to focus on the nursery door. A sensation that the dream was just out of reach was growing stronger. Just when Julianne thought she would remember, the room was filled with the sharp smack of the nursery door slamming.

"Julianne?" She heard the fear in Nick's voice as he called loudly from the foyer.

"I'm okay!" She shouted back, "the wind blew the door shut, that's all!"

She hoped that was true.

A few minutes later, the dogs, fresh pig-ear treats in mouth, bounded up the master stairs. Nick carried two freshly poured glasses of 7-Up and a plate of saltines with cream cheese.

After a pleasant bath, during which Nick washed her back, massaged her shoulders, and fed her crackers, Julianne was ready for bed.

It was a little before ten PM when they settled under the covers both with a book in hand. It had been an exhausting few hours and they were both a little crabby so when Nick decided to put his foot down about Julianne getting the bed rest the doctor ordered, it rubbed her the wrong way. They never were a couple that argued much and even when they did, they remained calm and gentle with each other. This time was no exception.

"You are not getting out of bed until it is time to go to see Dr. Klein."

"A girl's gotta pee you know." Julianne said, crossing her arms in front of her chest. She was feeling a little pouty at the prospect of being bed ridden for three days.

"Granted, you can go pee but all your meals will be served in bed my dear wife, and our little exploration of the first floor has been delayed until further notice."

Too tired to really battle it out, Julianne decided to concede.

"Just as well, I am getting bigger by the minute, in a few hours I will be too big to get through the door anyway."

After a good night of undisturbed sleep, Julianne felt better. She didn't get sick again, and it was easier to breathe. She admitted to Nick that a day of rest had done her good. He had stayed with her, waited on her hand and foot, and made sure she remained entertained. He even went as far as lugging the TV upstairs to their bedroom. The first day of bed rest was actually pretty great.

The second day however, was not so great. The movies were re-running and she was tired of reading. Nick was busy working in the room next door, planning the master bath. He offered to stay with her again but truth be told, she was getting tired of having a baby sitter. She wanted to get out of bed so badly! Her legs were stiff and her shoulders ached from lack of motion.

Around noon, Nick took a break from the pounding and sawing and came in to the bedroom covered in sawdust.

"What would you like for lunch my love?" He asked, wiping his freshly washed hands on a small towel.

"What do we have down there?"

"Oh, the usual. Cold cuts, salad, frozen pizza... are you having a craving?"

"Yeah but you'd have to go get it." She said, looking up at him through her lashes.

"I don't know if it is a good idea to leave you here alone. What if something happens? You are still sick."

"I am still a little tired but I haven't been sick to my stomach for two days. Besides, you've got your cell, grab me mine out of my purse. If I need you I can call you."

"Hmm." Nick looked at her with uncertainty on his face. "Are you sure you are feeling okay?"

"Yes! I'm fine." Julianne smiled at his concern. "I really want Empress Chicken and Crab Rangoon. Please, please, please, please, please?" She clasped her hands together and hugged them to her chest in a begging posture.

"Alright! Alright!" Nick said laughing. "I'll be back in twenty minutes. Go ahead and call it in. I need to wash up a bit."

Julianne waited for him to pull out of the driveway before she called Hunan's Chinese Restaurant. She wanted him to have a short wait. She was trying to buy a little more time alone. After she hung up, she pulled the covers off and slipped out of bed.

She needed to move around! She took a few timid steps to test her legs. Her muscles were tight and her joints ached a bit but otherwise she felt fine. After a few meager stretches, she was ready to walk.

She decided she would wander down to the library and choose another selection of novels. She wasn't in the mood for any of the ones Nick had brought to her. She motioned the dogs to stay put, and dropped her cell phone in the pocket of her robe.

She moved cautiously down the grand staircase. As she reached the bottom, she caught movement from the corner of her eye. She turned to look at the front door, which was slowly swinging open. She flinched at first, unsure if someone was coming through it. She halted, her foot in mid step, dangling above the bottom stair.

The door swung toward her, opening just a couple of inches and stopped. She couldn't see behind it from her spot on the stairs. She might have been able to see it in the mirror across the hall but she didn't dare look at it after the incident with the man's reflection on the stairs.

She held her breathe, trying to hear if there was any sound coming from the small hall between the two sets of front doors. She didn't know what she expected to hear. After a few seconds of hearing her own heart pounding in her chest, and little else, she worked up the nerve to take the last step down and move across the foyer.

It was dark in the hall, both sets of doors were solid wood and the only light between them was a tall thin line, which seeped in from the windows in the living room.

She concentrated on that thin strip trying to make out a shape or see movement. There seemed to be something there, just beyond the reach of the light. Her chest went cold as if her blood, thick with fright, was no longer pumping warmly through her veins. She could feel her breathing turn rapid and shallow as she caught sight of a tiny spot of light. It seemed to be reflecting off of something white and shiny that was apparently dangling in mid air.

She wrinkled her brow and squinted, trying to focus in on it. It was convex; the outwardly curving surface reflected the light the way a glass or a mug would, but it seemed wet or reflective.

Her curiosity getting the better of her, she took a step toward the door. Just as her hand lifted toward the doorknob the shiny white surface disappeared and reappeared.

Did it blink?

It was an eye! Someone was standing in the dark between the two sets of doors looking at her! Julianne took two steps backwards and bumped into the edge of the doorway into the living room. She sucked in a surprised breath preparing to scream but it stuck in her weakened lungs. The room started to dim and become cloudy around the peripheral of her vision. She was no longer focused on her surroundings, she was panicking at the thought Nick would come home to a stranger in the house.

"No!" She tried to shout but the word came out in a breathless whisper. She tried again, hearing her voice crack with panic. "No...no... please leave me alone." She was hyperventilating.

The door began to swing open again and Julianne's circle of vision became smaller and smaller, quickly fading to black.

Chapter Seven

Nick pulled into the driveway a little too quickly, causing the Jeep to jolt. The large bag of Chinese food nearly toppled from the seat. He could hear the gravel from beneath the tires pinging the under-carriage of the car before spinning off into the yard.

"Have to remember that when I go to mow the grass." He said quietly aloud to himself.

He was nervous. He shouldn't have left Jules alone, he had a really bad feeling that something was wrong. He jerked the car to a stop, grabbed up the brown paper bag full of Chinese delight and headed quickly in through the kitchen door.

"Jules! I'm home!" He ascended the back staircase taking the stairs two at a time. "Jules? You want to eat in the bedroom or downstairs?"

Julianne didn't answer and his level of concern leapt. He took the last three stairs at once, setting the bag of food down at the top as he nearly sprinted down the long hall towards the bedroom. He turned the corner and found the bed empty.

"Julianne?" He shouted even louder, a note of apprehension finding its way into his tone. "Julianne! Where are you?"

He looked back down the hall, the bathroom door was open and the light was out. He quickly moved through the bedroom to the adjoining nursery and that is where he found his wife, unconscious, curled up inside the babies' crib.

"Oh my God!" He rushed to her and struggled to lower the side of the crib and grabbed his wife under the neck and knees and lifted her from the baby bed.

He carefully carried her to their bed and laid her gently down. He was panicking. He wasn't sure what to do. He shook her gently, calling her name, his voice almost cracking with fear. She didn't open her eyes. He leaned down and put his head on her chest to listen if he could hear her heart beating.

As he did so, she let out a little moan. He looked up at her face and watched as her eyelids fluttered open.

"Oh thank God!" He sobbed with relief.

Chapter Eight

"Nick?" Julianne was confused. "What happened? I was... OH NO! Nick, I think there is someone in the house! Quick, call the police!"

She scrambled into a sitting position as she frantically whispered the command to Nick. When he didn't immediately respond, she reached over his shoulder toward the nightstand to grab the phone herself.

"Why do you think that?" Nick's tone and stance became immediately defensive, he turned to look at the bedroom door.

"I saw.... Something." Julianne was still hazy and she felt foolish telling Nick she fainted over an eye.

"What? What did you see?" Nick was almost shouting. His pulse was thumping through his muscles, he was ready to spring. If there was someone in the house, he and the dogs were going to take care of it.

"Wait. What makes you believe there is someone in the house?" Nick could feel the hair on the back of his neck beginning to rise.

"Because I saw him... or at least his eye. I think it was a he. I don't know for sure. Whoever it was, they were standing in the dark behind the inner set of front doors. All I could see was a reflection off the white of an eye!"

"An eye? How do you know it was an eye?"

"It blinked, Nick. I was looking at it, trying to figure out what it was and it blinked. I must have fainted. Did you carry me up here?"

"Uh..." he slipped the phone from his wife's hand, "No. I didn't actually. I found you asleep in the babies' crib."

"What?" She nearly shouted in alarm. "Then that proves it! There must have been someone here! The last thing I remember was standing in the doorway to the living room. You have to call the police!"

"Wait... where are the dogs?" Nick looked around the bedroom and found that they were not in any of their usual spots.

"Uh, I don't know. I left them here when I went down to get a book."

"What were you thinking?" He realized his tone was harsh but she was freaking him out.

"I just needed to stretch my legs. Go find the dogs. Nick please, I am worried. You can lecture me about getting out of bed later." She looked at him imploringly, real concern reflecting in her eyes.

"You going to be okay alone for a minute?"

"Yeah, just find them. Try calling them first."

Nick stepped out into the hall, gave two sharp whistles, the signal for the dogs to come. He waited, listening for the sound of their toenails clicking on the hard wood floors. At first, he could not hear anything, but as he took a few steps farther down the hall, he could hear three distinct barks. It was Atlas barking. He looked back at Julianne.

"You stay put, I will be right back."

"Do you hear them?"

"Yeah. I heard Atlas barking, sounds like he might be outside."

"What about Asia?"

"I don't know. I can't hear her. I will go find out, you stay here."

"Don't worry about that, I've had enough adventure for one day."

Nick walked as quietly as he could down the hall, trying to listen for Atlas to bark again. When he got to the top of the kitchen stairs, he whistled again. Again he heard three barks. He jogged quietly down the stairs, trying to figure out where it was coming from.

He got to the kitchen, paused and waited but Atlas didn't bark again. He looked out the door to the back yard, but didn't see either dog. He went to the door that led out front to the large carport but he wasn't there either.

"Atlas?" He called.

Another set of three barks came from behind him. He whirled around, and spotted the door to the basement. He walked over to it, listening. He could hear the sound of dog paws, knocking at the door. He unlatched the deadbolt and opened the door.

Atlas came rushing into the kitchen, tail wagging, obviously happy to be free of the basement. Asia followed directly behind and to Nick's surprise, a third dog came along, tail wagging right along with the other two.

All three dogs, turned and sat, looking at Nick as if they were expecting something. The odd dog seemed to be taking his or her cue from Atlas.

"Well, hello there. Who might you be?" Nick asked the strange new dog. Much to his delight, the dog offered a paw to be shaken, as if to say 'nice to meet you.'

The four of them traveled up the stairs and back down the long hall to the master bedroom where he found Julianne, wide eyed and waiting for him. She was so thrilled to see the two family dogs, she did not immediately notice the stray.

At least not until he or she headed around to the side of the bed, sat quietly and waited for her to finish petting the other two dogs, who had rushed right up onto the bed with her. Once they had settled, Julianne looked up, noticed the small black and white Collie waiting politely for her attention.

"What is this?" Julianne asked, looking at Nick.

He just shrugged and nodded back at the dog, which was waiting, paw extended for Julianne to shake.

"I don't know where that one came from. I found them all locked in the basement."

"In the basement? Someone was definitely here. I saw an eye, the dogs get locked in the basement and we end up with a strange dog? In the house? Something weird is definitely going on and I want to get a paper trail started just in case we get burglarized or vandalized... or worse." She said.

"I am wondering if whoever is here was here before. Remember the thud and the tie clasp we found at the bottom of the stairs?" Nick replied.

"That's right! Oh my God! Someone could have been coming and going all week! We need to change the locks today and get the cops out here to look around. Someone may still be here Nick!" Julianne was getting herself worked up.

"I agree. Something is going on. I don't know if a paper trail will help but it certainly cannot hurt."

"What do you mean? Don't you believe me that I saw an intruder?" She asked defensively.

"Oh no, I believe you but I don't think we are dealing with an intruder. I think we might be the intruders."

"What do you mean?" Jules was frowning at her husband, looking at him as though he suddenly began speaking in a foreign language.

He couldn't blame her, he knew what he was about to say would sound crazy but he had to fess up to what had been nagging at the back of his mind ever since the night of the power failure.

"Jules, you might think I am nuts, but I think this house might be haunted and I think the ghosts are trying to send us a message."

Chapter Nine

Nick called his new friend Josh McNett, who was a beat officer on the St. Joseph Police force. They had met about a week ago at a storm chaser class. Nick had taken the class for kicks, thinking he would never actually get out and chase a tornado around. He hoped he wasn't abusing their new friendship by calling but Julianne clearly wasn't convinced that there was anything other than a flesh and blood intruder in their house.

He didn't think there was any good in it but he called in hopes that it would calm Julianne down. He called Josh because he at least felt he would keep it quiet for the time being.

"Well? Are they going to send a unit over? Can they dust for prints, see if they can determine if it is a known criminal? What about police protection, can they give us protection?"

Nick sat down on the edge of the bed next to his wife. He pulled her close and held her until she was no longer shaking. It was as if what he said had not even registered. When he felt she was reasonably calm he tilted her face up to his own and looked her in the eyes.

"Did you hear what I said Jules?"

"What about the place being haunted?" She scoffed.

"Uh huh."

"Nick, come on. You don't really think that do you?"

"Well, it might not hurt to contact a priest. I don't know whom else we would call in a situation like this..."

"Situation like this?" She sounded irritated. "A situation like this is simple. We have an intruder. We don't need a priest, we need a cop!" She was nearly shouting.

Nick decided not to push it. He wanted her to remain calm.

"Well, Josh is going to send a car over with a couple of patrol officers to check the place out but he feels pretty sure that our dogs would be alerting if anyone was still here.

Even so, being a friend he can arrange to have the night shift swing by a couple of times a night and check things out. He said that is usually enough to discourage someone from casing a place or vandals from destroying anything."

"I wish there was more they could do." Jules sounded terribly disappointed.

"Hey." He said, putting a gentle hand beneath his wife's chin and lifting her face to look him in the eye again. "I will protect you. I am sorry I left you today. I won't be leaving you again until we are certain the place is safe. I will call a locksmith right now and get the locks changed. Should I call Animal Control to pick up our strange friend here?"

"Oh, I dunno, she seems to be getting along with the others and seems very well mannered with the way she introduced herself to me."

"She? How do you know it's a she?"

"I don't really, just that she looks like a she. See if she will let you check..." Jules chuckled at the idea of her husband having to peep at the privates of an unknown dog. But as if the dog understood their conversation, she rolled over onto her back and confirmed she was indeed a female dog and apparently wanted Nick to rub her tummy.

"There's a good girl." He said giving her a good scratch. "She seems clean, not like a stray. I know she wasn't in the basement before; it is just so odd that someone would break in and leave her here like that.

Maybe someone wanted to give her a good home. Maybe that is what this is all about."

"I think your reaching a bit but I don't see any reason to send her to jail. She is obviously really smart."

"This is the weirdest thing I have ever seen Nick."

"Me too Jules. I just hope we can still say that tomorrow."

Chapter Ten

The officers were looking at Julianne like she was certifiable. They were not at all convinced that she was telling them the truth. They started off okay. They had asked her to explain exactly what she had seen of the intruder.

"Well, I didn't really see him... or her... probably a him, he was taller than me."

"How do you know that the intruder was taller than you if you didn't see anyone?" The younger of the two officers asked her.

"Well, I could see an...." She paused and looked at Nick. He gave the slightest shake of his head, indicating that she should not tell them about the eye.

"I saw a shadow I guess. It was just a sense I had of the person being taller."

"Did you hear a voice or see any facial details that might get us looking in the right direction?" The older officer asked.

"No. I fainted as soon as I realized someone was there." She looked down at her hands, which, were folded neatly in her lap.

She was sitting on the sofa in the living room surrounded by mountains of boxes, some empty, some still full.

"Officer McNett mentioned you think the intruder might have been here before?"

"We've heard sounds. Someone on the stairs and there is the dog..." She trailed off suddenly feeling foolish.

They had nothing to give the officer's that would help them find a suspect. The younger officer, a dark headed man who couldn't have been more than thirty, was looking at Julianne like he thought she was nuts.

Nick was growing frustrated. He had anticipated the confusion on the part of the police but he had not counted on the condescension.

"What dog?" The older officer asked. He was in his late fifties, white hair and pale eyes. He was looking at Julianne with compassion. He at least felt empathy for her, even if he did believe she was wasting their time.

"I came home and found a stray in the house." Nick cut in, stepping forward from the doorway where he had been leaning.

"We thought perhaps the intruder left her behind but I doubt she will give us any information." He was ready to end the interview when the younger man asked if they could see the dog.

"You never know Mister Sullivan, she might have an identity chip. We can at least look her over."

"Sure. No problem, I will go get her." He'd settled the strange little dog into the nursery with food water and blankets. He didn't want to take the chance that the dogs would discover a difference of opinion while the police were there, upsetting Julianne with a fit of snarls and bites.

"Mind if I go with you?" The older of the two officers asked.

Nick didn't like the idea of leaving Julianne alone with the younger man. He was not being kind and she had been under enough stress, but he didn't want them to think they were hiding something so he agreed to have the officer follow him.

They ascended the master stairs in silence, Nick taking the lead. As he reached the top he waited for the officer to make the last few steps before he opened the door to the nursery.

He flipped on the light expecting to find the dog curled up on the pile of blankets he had left with her earlier. She wasn't there. He stepped inside, scanning the length of the room.

"Hmm. That's odd." He said turning to confirm that the door to the master bedroom was still closed. "Here girl."

The officer, whose name badge identified him as Officer Barnes, looked behind the stack of boxes in the corner. The dog was no where to be found.

"I don't understand..." Nick said, bewildered at the dog's disappearance.

"I think I might." Officer Barnes peered out the open nursery door and then shut it.

"What?" Nick was perplexed.

"Have other thing's been going on?"

"What kind of things do you mean?" Nick wasn't sure if he was alluding to a haunting or perhaps thought he and Jules might be on drugs.

"Oh... you know... bumps in the night kind of things."

Nick exhaled, rubbing his face. He was tired and still dirty from working on the bathroom. He couldn't gauge Officer Barnes' reason for asking but he was too tired to tell the man anything other that the truth.

"Yes. We have had a couple of strange things happen but that doesn't explain where the dog went." Nick said, leaning back against the dresser.

"Did your dogs object to the stray dog's presence?"

"No. In fact they didn't seem…." Nick's words trailed off. He felt a cold chill sweep down his spine as he realized what the other man was getting at.

"Like they didn't even know she was there." Barnes finished his sentence in a quiet, sympathetic tone.

"This is crazy. You think our house is being haunted by a dog?"

"Honestly, I wouldn't even venture a guess. That kind of thing is more my sister's territory."

"Your sister? What does she do?"

"She is a sensitive. She can walk into a place and gets a psychic vibe or something. She might be able to tell you what is going on better than I or Officer Norris can."

"How can I contact her?" Nick was willing to try anything at this point.

"Here, her number," he pulled a page out of his notebook and handed it to Nick. "She doesn't usually answer if she doesn't recognize the call so be sure to leave a message and give her your address. She's been interested in this place for a long time."

They left the nursery and headed back down to where they left Julianne and Officer Norris. Julianne was still on the couch but the officer had stepped out onto the front porch and was inspecting the lock on the front door.

Nick and Barnes joined him there.

"No sign of forced entry. What did you get off the dog?"

"Nothing. She is just a mutt, not the kind of animal you'd spend money putting an ID tag on."

"Well, then I guess that wraps it up. I have your wife's statement, we will open a file on it. We'll cruise by a couple times tonight, check out the property and make sure everything looks all right."

"Thanks officers. We appreciate that."

Nick watched the officers leave. Barnes had turned and nodded at him as he had opened his car door, as if to say 'tomorrow.' Nick had no idea how he was going to convince Julianne to let this woman into their house.

Chapter Eleven

After making her tea and talking calmly to her about security systems and changing locks, he had put his distraught wife to bed. He'd picked up the food and blankets he had left for the Collie, and had looked around again for a way that she could have escaped the confines of the nursery. He'd found nothing.

He'd taken his own dogs on a final check of the house. He wanted to be sure all the windows had working locks and all the doors were bolted. He talked softly to Atlas and Asia, sure they had been feeling the tension in the air.

"Don't worry pups. This is all going to seem very silly tomorrow."

He wasn't sure if he was trying to convince them or himself. He didn't want to think about an invisible man following him around, watching his every move. He was on the verge of losing it, but felt like he had to keep it under control for Jules.

He managed to stay calm until he joined Jules in bed. He had even caught an hour or two of sleep before waking up with a terrible taste in his mouth, and an aching thirst. Getting that glass of water from the bathroom had been the last normal thing he had done.

From the moment he switched off the light, his world had turned upside down. Something had lured him down to the kitchen so that it could attack Julianne. The blue light in the kitchen, the stunning shock, the locked bedroom door was all forgotten in this moment. Something was wrong with his wife.

"Come on Jules. Take a breath. Please baby take a breath!"

He whispered urgently to his wife while listening for any sign of shallow breathing. He checked her pulse. It was slow and irregular. He tilted her head back and forced air into her lungs, trying desperately to will her to breathe. He pumped her chest five times and then more mouth to mouth. He talked to her while he did further compressions.

"You cannot die. Julianne do you hear me? I cannot raise these babies without you. I would be lost without you. Please breathe!" He was sobbing, tears rolling down his face dripping onto his wife's cheek.

"Dear God... please don't take her away from me. I need her. The babies need her. Please... please... please!"

After what seemed like an eternity, Nick could hear the faint sound of sirens. He listened for a second, then said "You hear that Jules? That's help baby! Just stay with me!"

He continued the breathing until he could see the reflection of the red and blue ambulance lights dancing in through his bedroom window. As he lifted Julianne from the floor, he could hear the paramedics trying to decide the best way to gain entry to the house.

He moved as quickly as he could, with two concerned dogs shadowing his every move, heading down the main staircase. He looked at Julianne as they descended. She was so pale and limp in his arms. Something was definitely not right. She was in trouble and needed to get to the hospital.

Nick was consumed by fear for his wife. All the events of the evening were long forgotten as he placed her on the gurney. He was overwhelmed by the sight of her pale skin and couldn't collect his thoughts. He could not feel the strain of his muscles ease, or the ache of his back, or the pain in his lungs. He did feel a little relieved that help was here, and Julianne had a chance.

Chapter Twelve

The EMTs were calm and efficient. They immediately took over CPR and simultaneously wheeled Jules into the bus. Nick followed them into the ambulance, watching for any sign of life in his wife's face.

"Don't worry sir. You did a great job while you were waiting. You did everything you could for her, the breathing and the compressions were good and the blanket was smart. Kept her from going into shock. There is no doubt in my mind that you gave her a fighting chance but now I need for you to let us do our thing okay?"

"What?" Nick looked up at the man, confused for a moment as to what he meant.

"Oh!" He realized he was leaning over Julianne, restricting their access to her.

He jolted back against the side of the ambulance, horrified at the realization that he was being intrusive. He stayed there, watching in terror as they intibated his wife.

The ride to the hospital took less than fifteen minutes, but to Nick a lifetime passed. He couldn't take his eyes off Julianne's pale skin and her utterly still face. He had never seen her less animated.

When they arrived at the emergency room, Nick was allowed to run along side the gurney until they reached the triage center. At once a team of gown clad medical personal swarmed the gurney. Nick was pushed aside by a short but persistent Latina woman. He tried to step around her but she stopped him more with the tone of her voice than the hand she placed in the center of his chest.

"Sir. Sir!" She waited until she had eye contact with him. "I need to get some information. First, how far along is your wife?"

"Uh... seven months." Nick had to pull his attention away from the buzzing herd of people with Julianne. They were wheeling her away, and Nick once again tried to side step the small woman.

"Sir!" She said loudly in an even sharper tone. "You need to listen to me... what is your name?"

"Uh... Nick. Nick Sullivan, that woman is my wife Julianne. She is seven months pregnant with twins."

"Has she had any complications with the pregnancy?"

"What? No." Nick was distracted as they wheeled Julianne out of sight.

"Mr. Sullivan?" She waited again for him to meet her eyes.

"Mister Sullivan...Nick... the best thing you can do for your wife right now is answer a few more questions. That group of people who just wheeled her away is the top OB team we've got. The EMTs radioed ahead and we were prepared for her arrival. She is getting the best possible care but we need to know what we are dealing with. Do you understand?"

Her tone was softer, more sensitive and it calmed Nick's fear enough for him to nod and focus on her questions.

"Has she been sick or is she taking any medications?"

"Yeah, she was here the day before yesterday. The doctor said she was presenting symptoms of the flu."

"What prompted you to bring her in?"

"Uh... she was dreaming. I couldn't get her to wake up and she was pale. Not as pale as tonight..." Nick's voice caught, an unexpected bubble of emotion rose in his throat.

"It's okay Mister Sullivan, she is in the best place possible right now. Where there any other symptoms?"

"Well, she was sick to her stomach and had trouble breathing."

"Okay, I need to take this information to the team who's running tests on her. You stay put, there are chairs over there."

She pointed to a small group of chairs in a corner of the room. Two very sullen and exhausted looking men occupied a couple of the chairs. The older of the two men was gripping the shoulder of the younger man, talking quietly to him. *Father and son*, Nick thought.

Feeling helpless and in complete despair, Nick sat slowly down into the chair farthest from the two men. He dropped his head into his hands, trying desperately to bite back on the tears that lingered just below the surface. He didn't want to cry in front to these two strangers.

A few minutes later, Nick looked up when he felt a light tap on his shoulder. The older gentleman, who Nick now noticed was a priest, was holding two cups of coffee.

Nick looked around, the other man had left without his having noticed. He met the Priest's eyes and almost came undone. He saw real compassion and kindness in them.

"You look like you could use this," he said.

"Thanks." Nick reached for the warm cup, not really interested in drinking it.

"Father Donohue," he said extending his free hand to Nick.

"Nick Sullivan. Nice to meet you Father. Will you sit down?" Nick indicated the chair next to him.

The Priest sat, and at first neither man spoke. Nick wanted very badly to ask him questions but did not know where to begin. Father Donohue broke the ice for him.

"Something is troubling you?" It was a question.

"Yes Father. My extremely pregnant wife almost quit breathing on me tonight. It really freaked me out."

"I think it would frighten any man. How far along is she?"

"Seven months. She is carrying twins, Father. I am worried that the strain is going to be too much for her."

"Many generations of women have carried twins. Keep the faith, your wife is young and healthy?"

"Yeah. Had a touch of the flu the last couple of days but so far the pregnancy has been smooth sailing."

"Well there you have it. She is young and strong and you two are obviously very much in love. She has a lot to hang on to. She is likely dehydrated. Have faith that it will turn out exactly as it is supposed to."

"What if this wasn't God's plan?" Nick asked, his heart beating a little faster.

"What do you mean? I believe most things are part of God's plan."

"Most, but not all?"

"No. Not all. There is inherent evil in this world. Occasionally it wins a small battle against good."

"Do you believe in spirits, Father?"

"You mean spirits, as in souls?"

"No." Nick hesitated, glancing up to meet the priest's eyes. "No, I mean spirits as in ghosts."

"Do you?" The priest's tone remained neutral.

"Never in my life, Father. But now..."

"Has something been happening where you live?"

"Yeah. We just moved into the Frederick Mansion, you know, behind The Immaculate Conception?"

"Ah yes, I see."

"You do?"

"I have heard the history of the house. I know that the neighborhood considers it haunted. Maybe hearing the legend, in conjunction with being in a new home, has your imagination working over time?"

"Well, I thought so at first Father. But now..." He didn't finish his sentence but his gaze turned to the corner where he last had sight of his wife.

"Well son, I know the Church acknowledges the existence of evil in many forms. I cannot discount that there may be evil in the form of energy we cannot understand. Perhaps you should arrange to have the house blessed. I have often heard that it helps in these types of situations."

"Yes Father. Perhaps I should. Thank you for your advice."

"Just have faith in The Lord. He won't let you down."

Just as the Priest stood to leave, the small powerful woman who'd spoken to him earlier came back around the corner.

"How is she?" Nick stood as she approached.

"She is stable for now. She has not regained consciousness just yet. We need to do a series of tests, I need your consent."

"What kind of tests?"

"We need to get film of her heart. There is a minimal risk to the twins. It *is* minimal and the doctor feels it is absolutely necessary."

Nick rubbed his hand through his hair and looked at the forms the woman had handed him. He nodded and clicked the pen.

"Sign here. Don't worry, they will take all precaution."

Nick signed the paperwork and prayed that he was doing the right thing. Julianne would never forgive him if he let them do something that harmed the twins. He just hoped they were able to find out what was wrong with her before she got any worse.

After several grueling hours in the uncomfortable waiting room chair, the nurse finally came back to speak with him. He rose as she rounded the corner, taking several steps forward to shorten the distance.

"Mr. Sullivan, your wife and babies are fine."

"Oh! Thank God."

"We did however find a condition called Mitral Valve Stenosis. It is a narrowing of the heart valve. It is something she has had all her life but it usually doesn't cause symptoms until the body comes under stress. Pregnancy, especially twins, qualifies."

"What does that mean? Can you fix it?"

"Eventually, your wife may need surgery but it is not critical yet so we will wait till after the delivery of the twins."

"What is the risk to Julianne if you wait?"

"There is some risk but she will be admitted to the hospital and monitored during the duration of the pregnancy. We will keep her on low sodium diet and keep her hydrated. We will have the twins on a fetal monitor. We will give her a special round of antibiotics before the delivery to prevent bacteria from building up in her heart."

"Jesus. Bacteria in her heart?" Nick was in shock.

"Worst case scenario: her condition worsens and we have to take the twins via cesarean section and perform the surgery immediately after."

"But she's only seven months. Isn't that dangerous for the twins?" Nick's head was spinning. He was starting to breathe too fast. He sat down in the nearest chair.

"There is always risk with premature babies. However, by seven months they will have really good lung and heart function so the risk in this case would be minimal."

"You keep saying that. Minimal risk." Nick's tone was becoming hard. "It doesn't feel minimal when it is your wife and children on the line.

"I cannot promise you that your loved ones will all come out of this okay, but I can promise you that you have a top notch team doing everything they can to make sure they do. Your family is in good hands Mr. Sullivan."

Nick covered his face with his hands. He needed to block the reality out for a minute. He needed to calm himself. He needed to see his wife. After a moment, he looked up.

"Can I see Julianne?"

"Yes but only for a few minutes. We have given her a sedative to keep her calm. You can come back in the morning for a few hours and then again around dinner. Follow me and I will show you to your wife's room."

Nick followed the woman down the hall and into the Intensive Care Unit. She opened the door and motioned for him to enter a room right across from the nurse's station. He entered the room and paused to let his eyes adjust. The curtains were drawn over the window that overlooked the corridor. The only light in the room was a small neon strip light, which hung above and behind his wife's bed.

"Remember, only stay a few minutes. She needs to sleep." The nurse reminded him before shutting the door.

"Oh Jules..." Nick's voice came out in a shaky whisper.

Julianne's eyes were closed and her face looked so incredibly pale in the harsh white light. Nick took a deep breath to repress the emotion that was rising in his chest. He needed to be strong for Julianne. He had to keep it together so she wouldn't get too worried and cause herself undue stress.

Nick pulled a chair from the wall and slid it next to the bed. He sat down and took his wife's cold pale hand in his own. It was cold in the room. He knew Julianne would hate that. He glanced at her still form, his eyes coming to rest on her feet. He made a mental note to ask a nurse to get her an extra blanket for her feat.

"Hey…" A shallow replica of his wife's voice whispered.

Nick looked at Julianne and saw that her golden green eyes were open. He half sobbed, half laughed with relief. He raised her hand to his lips and kissed it several times.

"Hello there." His voice was full of gratitude.

"What happened?"

"You uh… tried to quit breathing on me. You're in the ICU. You and the babies are fine. You've been here a while, and they have run a bunch of tests."

"What did they do?"

"Oh, you know, they looked at your heart and head and the babies. There was a lot of medical mumbo jumbo, but basically they found a narrow heart valve. Nothing critical but you may have to have surgery after the twins are born."

"Surgery? On my heart?"

"Don't worry too much about that right now. You'll be talking to a cardiologist who can explain it to you. It isn't real bad right now so you aren't in any immediate danger from it."

"Well that's good I guess. When will they send in a doctor?" Julianne's speech was becoming slower with an airy quality to it.

"Look honey, I do have some bad news. The doctors want you to stay in the hospital until the twins are born. Don't worry though, I will be here to entertain you every second they let me. Okay?"

"Okay..." Julianne's eyes had been slowly blinking. Opening less and less with each blink, Nick didn't know if she would even remember the conversation.

"I have to go honey. They won't let me stay tonight but I will be back in the morning. I love you Jules." Nick bent down and kisses his wife's forehead.

"You...too." Julianne was already asleep by the time the last word passed her lips.

Nick stood up, returned the chair to its spot on the wall. He bent down and kissed his wife's cheek. He brushed her hair out of her eyes and pulled the thin blanket a little higher. He would try to be back before she woke up in the morning. In the meantime he had errands to run.

Chapter Thirteen

Nick sat in the driveway looking at the house. He juggled what the nurse had told him over in his mind. She had said that the condition his wife had was something she had been suffering from for a long time. *Then why do I feel like blaming this God damned house?*

Checking his watch, Nick decided that six thirty was not too late to call the detective's sister. He pulled the folded slip of paper out of his wallet. The detective had scrawled his sister's name and number in a tight, neat, efficient hand.

Savana Williams
816-523-8098

Nick dialed the number with shaking hands. He took several deep breaths while listening to the line ring. To his surprise, a woman answered.

"Savana Williams." The voice was soft and friendly. Nick felt his tension abate slightly.

"Ms. Williams. My name is Nick Sullivan, have I caught you at a good time?"

"Sure Mr. Sullivan, Jason... uh... Detective Barnes... called me. You're the couple who just moved into the old Frederick Smith mansion on Messanie right?"

"Yes. That's right. He said you might be able to help us out. You're a sensitive?"

"I am a psychic Mr. Sullivan. My brother uses the term 'sensitive' because he thinks it carries less taboo."

"Psychic. Right." Nick suddenly wondered what he was doing.

"Relax Mr. Sullivan, it is okay to be a skeptic. It's healthy in fact. But if you would like, I would be very interested in coming out to your place and taking a look around, see if I pick up on anything."

Deciding that he had nothing to loose at this point and feeling like he had to do *something* to help Julianne he made an appointment with Savana to come to the house early in the afternoon the next day. It would be between visiting hours, he would not tell Julianne until he heard what the psychic had to say.

When he arrived at the hospital the next morning, Julianne was already awake. She rewarded his early arrival with a loving smile. He was relieved to see that the color had returned to her face and she was sitting up in bed.

"I guess they told you that I am a captive for now." She said with a half-hearted smile.

"Yeah… they mentioned it. Did they fill you in on the heart valve thing?"

"Yeah. Kinda weird. They said it has been narrowing slowly most of my life. Kinda feels like my own heart is conspiring against me."

"No. Don't look at it that way. Your heart is just so full of love that it had to close up a bit to keep it from spilling out too fast." Nick kissed his wife's hand.

He stayed with her for the allowed three hours. He made a visit to the flower shop and bought her a movie card so she could watch movies on-demand on the large plasma TV in her room. He also picked up a pair of pale yellow stuffed bears that were locked in a hug.

Their super soft materials made them perfect for when the twins were born.

He was staggered by the concept of having two small lives depending on him to protect them and their mother. He felt the pressure to have a plan more than ever. He was doing fine, an architect with a good reputation, but he always felt like he was waiting for the day his luck would run out. He prayed that this was not that day.

As he drove back to the house, he wondered again if he was doing the right thing by meeting with a psychic. He came to the conclusion that he had no reason to not let the woman in. It really couldn't hurt.

He pulled into the driveway, fifteen minutes before the scheduled meeting but there was already a strange vehicle in his drive. He pulled along side the white Suburban, looked in the window but there was no one in the driver's seat. He went ahead and pulled his car into the carport and parked.

When he got out of the car, he could hear footsteps coming down the path that led in front of the house. He stepped out of the carport and found a woman in her late forties, blonde, thin and attractive for her age. She smiled and waved at him as she approached.

"Mr. Sullivan! Pleasure to meet you. Savana Williams, please call me Savana. I hope you don't mind, I wanted to walk the grounds before I started in the house, just to get a feel for the property."

"Did you sense anything?"

"Yes. There has been a lot of grief here. Not just trauma, though I do feel that, but grief. A lot of it, as if people were grieving here for years. I don't really understand it."

Nick decided not to tell her about the map he had found in the library. It indicated that there may have been a cemetery on the land at one point, which would be consistent with years of grief, but he decided not to give her any information.

"Well, if you're ready, we can head inside." Nick said instead.

"Great. I don't mind telling you, I have wanted to visit this place. I played here as a little girl with the children that used to live here. I was sensitive then but didn't understand what I was feeling. Ever since I have been researching paranormal phenomena, I have wanted to come back and see if I felt as strongly as I did then."

"Well, your wait is over, I guess." Nick nodded toward the kitchen door. He unlocked it and swung it open. He called for the dogs, and they came bounding down the back stairs, tails wagging.

He introduced Savana to the dogs and then took them out to the run he had constructed the evening before. He had been up stringing the chain link well after 10 PM. He hadn't been in any real hurry to get back inside. Luckily, the hard work he'd put in building the run had sufficiently worn him out, and he fell asleep quickly. He slept hard and sound all night, nothing having wrested him from his sleep.

When he got back into the house, Savana was standing very still, staring into the entrance of the pantry. He almost asked her if she would like something to eat but he realized she was not aware of him. Her face was animated and her eyes were darting around the small, shelved room. It looked to Nick as though she was watching something he could not see.

Chapter Fourteen

Please God No! It was what kept running through her head over and over again. She didn't want to believe it was happening. She had been aware of the mister's attentions but assumed it would be a few lewd stares and a pat or two on the rump and he would move on to someone else.

But that did not happen. Now she was trapped in the pantry with her wrists painfully pinned in one of his fat pink hands while the other hand was ripping at her skirt. She fought him but he was such a big man and she was such a small woman. She didn't stand a chance.

"I've seen you wagging your tail at me girl! What did you think? You could tease me forever and never pay a price for it?" He grunted at her as he fumbled at her laces.

"No sir! I didn't! I never..."

Her screams were cut short as his meaty fist swiped hard across her mouth. She could taste blood mingled with her tears. She had bit her tongue. In her momentary daze, she quit struggling. It was the opportunity he needed to violently force his hand inside her clothing and viciously push a finger into her. The pain of it brought her back to her senses and she managed one bellowing scream before he covered her mouth with his.

He jammed his tongue into her cheek, trying to forge a kiss out of the struggle. He had her underclothes ripped away. He pulled his fingers from within her and struggled with the ties of his own trousers. He almost lost grip of her in his anticipation.

She wrenched one hand free of his painful grasp and raked her fingernails across his face. It was a pathetic attempt at self-defense and she knew it. He became enraged and his struggles became more violent. He ripped his own trousers down and forced himself into her. He grunted and panted as he pushed hard to get his member inside her, but she was unused and dry.

Nanette began to sob loudly, punctuated with a sharp cry of pain, as he achieved his goal. She quit struggling. It didn't matter anymore. She was ruined. The shock of it made her numb with fear. She almost fainted when she heard him cry out in surprise. He was yanked backward off of her and she slid from the counter to the floor.

Her eyes were glazed over and she could barely make out the form of the gardener as he stood pummeling the man of the house. She tried to stand, but slipped in her blood. She grabbed the edge of the counter and watched as the round, old, greedy man retrieved a pistol from the pocket of his overcoat. She opened her mouth to warn Henry, but before she got the chance she heard the loud crack of gunfire.

She screamed and fell back to the floor, curling up into a small ball, trying to disappear into the dust of the floor. She didn't dare look up; she could hear the gardener struggling for breath, a horrible sucking sound accompanied by groans of pain. Her heart broke. He had tried to save her and had paid with his life.

And now she would pay too.

She could barely hear the sound of the mister's curses over the roar of the blood that was rushing through her ears.

"You evil temptress!" He screamed at her, kicking her with his hard soles of his boots.

"Please..." she sobbed.

"You dare beg me after the mess you have created! You are the spawn of the devil! This is your fault you Creole bitch! Now a man is dead and you will pay for his life with your own!"

She looked through the strands of her rumpled hair just in time to see him level the revolver at her. She felt the heat explode in her chest and side before she heard the shot. She struggled to get to her feet. She could no longer hear his raging words.

Her ears were ringing from the blast of the pistol and the pain was like nothing she had ever known. Life was draining from her; she could feel herself going cold and numb.

She used the reprieve from the pain to get her wits about her. She could see the mister, standing in the kitchen, fumbling to return his clothes to order. She grabbed the edge of the counter and pulled herself upright. As she did so, she felt an odd draining sensation at her feet. As she steadied herself on the edge of the counter, she looked down. She was not prepared for what she would see. There, crumpled at her feet was the lifeless, pail, bleeding form of her own body.

Savana watched the antique drama unfold in front of her. She was oddly detached even though she could feel the pain and terror of the young woman. She was such a tiny creature with beautiful golden-olive skin. Her hair was long and dark, her face narrow and beautifully carved. Her lips, now stained with blood had been full and dark. He had called her a 'Creole bitch.' She had the look of it about her, and her voice sounded of it.

The sadness that overwhelmed Savana had her stumbling backward from the pantry and turning she nearly collided with Nick. He reached out a hand to steady her, his eyes as wide as saucers. She held up a hand to indicate that she was okay.

She took a few wobbly steps and sat at the large wooden banquet table that was near to the pantry. As she laid her palm on the top of the table, she had another brief vision.

Kimberly sat at the kitchen table waiting for her mother to finish talking to the lady with the bird. The bird was large and colorful and named Sadie. The cage had hung in the corner of the nursery where Kim slept and she was sad that the bird was leaving. She sat tracing circles on the surface of the table with her tiny chubby hands, pouting, hoping they would change their minds about taking the bird. Unexpectedly, the front door opened.

Kim, who was only four years old, could see the young blond-haired man who had come through the front door. Evidently the lady with the bird could not. This had happened before. The man, who looked to be younger than her mother, stood for a moment looking at her. She lifted her fingers in an uncertain wave. He winked at her before he turned and shut the door and tossed the deadbolt.

Kim turned as her mother addressed the man who had just entered.

"Quit it Hank! You're scaring my friend!" Her mother's voice was firm but there was an edge to it that Kimberly didn't like. She turned to look back at the man in the hallway. He was smiling at her, ignoring her mother as he tipped his hat to her and faded away.

The lady with the bird was talking rapidly about the lock turning on the door. "IT TURNED BY ITSELF! I like you Gail, I do, but really, how can you live here?"

She was upset. She snatched the birdcage off the table, causing a fray of feathers and squawking within the cage. She trotted as quickly as her shiny leather baby dolls would carry her. She was to the kitchen door and out onto the steps before Gail could finish pleading with her to stay.

"Really. It happens all the time. No one has ever been hurt!"

Her words trailed after her friend as she walked quickly across the drive, leaving the door open behind her.

Kimberly watched as her mother started to cry. This upset her even more than the disappearing bird. She threw her hands up over her eyes and dropped her head onto the table and cried, her tears soaking into the wood.

Savana felt the tears sliding down her own face. Her focus returned to the present and she looked at Nick who was sitting across from her at the large kitchen table. The same table that young Kimberly sat at while watching her mother cry. She quickly wiped the wetness from her cheeks and smiled at Nick who was the picture of concern and discomfort.

"There is a lot of energy in this house. It goes back to events that happened long ago and the effects rippled forward for a long time. This place has been active for a long time and the ghosts have disturbed many families in the meantime."

"You can tell all of that from walking into the kitchen?" Nick was astounded.

"I get energy from things I touch. When I touched the pantry door, I got a vision of a terrible death that occurred there. When I sat down at the table, I had a vision of a little girl and her mother being frightened by the ghost of a young man. I could see him through the eyes of the little girl, she was able to see more than her mother could."

"Someone died in the pantry?"

"Yes, a servant woman was being raped by her employer. It was interrupted by a gardener, and the man became angry and shot them both."

"Jesus. Are they the spirits that haunt the house?" Nick had let go of all skepticism.

"Yes, I believe that they are two of them."

This woman was either an amazing actress or she truly believed what she was telling him. He was suddenly anxious to know more. She might be able to find out if the ghosts or the house was somehow responsible for his wife's condition. He wanted to move to other rooms and see what she could find but he waited until she had regained her composure.

"Would you like something to drink?"

"No. Thank you. Can you tell me a little bit about what has been going on in the house?"

"Well, I had a bizarre encounter here in the kitchen with a blue light and phantom shock. The dogs have gone berserk, chasing and barking at something my wife and I cannot see. My wife has seen a reflection of a man in the mirror in the living room. A strange dog appeared and then disappeared. The nursery door slammed shut and now my wife has suddenly taken ill."

"You think the illness may have been brought on by an entity in the house?" Savana was clearly surprised by the idea.

"Do you think it is possible?"

"I don't know. I have never heard of anything like that exactly but the research into this field is still in its infancy."

"Can you communicate with the ghosts? Can you ask them?"

"I don't communicate directly with entities. I can often sense them when they are present and I can get visions and emotions if they touch me but I cannot communicate with them in any traditional sense."

"Would you like to continue the tour? Maybe something will come clear." The hope on Nick's face bordered on desperation.

Savana sincerely doubted that the souls who lingered in the house would choose to divulge any information to her that would reveal malice but Nick looked at her so pleadingly that she agreed to try.

As she moved through the house, Nick not far behind, she would momentarily be stunned into stillness by flashes of visions and emotions that belonged to owners long since gone from the house. It was a long, sad history of violence, poverty and death. It was a suffocating feeling that made Savana heavy and depressed. She could see how that could drive a person, living or dead, crazy if they lived with it for too long.

As they entered the master bedroom, she was bombarded anew with visions of a dying woman, surrounded by long faced, dirty children. Theirs was a story of disappointment and poverty. There were too many painful feelings swirling around her, awful visions of abuse and violation that had nothing to do with the paranormal. Except maybe, providing and emotionally charged environment that was ripe for paranormal activity. Savana felt dizzy under the weight of the sadness and sat down on the edge of the bed.

"Are you okay?" Nick asked.

"Yes," She replied, "just a little overwhelmed. Mind if I get that water now?"

"I've got bottled water down in the kitchen. Would you like to go back down?"

"No. I would like to stay here for a moment. Would you mind going to get it for me?"

Nick shifted his weight between his feet, rocking back and forth for a moment before answering. He was a bit reluctant to leave this stranger alone in his bedroom but he decided it would be worth the risk if she could really find out what was going on here.

Nick nodded and headed down the hall toward the back stairs. Savana closed her eyes, practicing a light form of mediation to re-center herself, and waited for the dizzy feeling to pass. When she felt calm and steady, she stood from the bed and walked to the door leading to the nursery. As she did so, the air became cooler and a buzz of electricity filled the room. As she passed through the door she was immediately struck with the feeling of being trapped.

She stood very still in the middle of the room, struggling to breathe normally. She could feel a familiar sensation coursing through her limbs, a weak electrical flow that pulsed with emotion much like the blood pulsing through her veins. It was a sensation that was always with her to some degree but became almost unbearable in places with a lot of emotional energy.

She closed her eyes, intending to meditate again but instead was greeted with the vision of two women, arguing. The younger woman was the woman whom she had witnessed being raped and murdered in the kitchen pantry down below. Savana listened very hard but their voices seemed to be in a vacuum. She could only catch pieces of words.

She took a deep breath and concentrated a bit harder. She could hear the voices getting louder. The vision of the two women wavered and then flickered out, but just before it did she clearly heard the older woman, a slightly plump, gray-haired woman dressed in some type of servants garb, say "...not the same mister!"

The voice had a pleading tone, it was clear the older woman was trying to convince the younger.

As Savana opened her eyes, the walls had closed her into a small box. It startled her and she immediately ducked, throwing her hands up. As she did so, the walls flung backward, returning to their previous state. It was enough to make her feel sick. She backed out of the room and returned to her seat on the edge of the bed.

Nick came through the door and handed her the bottle of water. "You okay?"

"Yes. Just had a disturbing moment alone in the nursery."

"What did you see?"

"Mostly I felt. There was so much emotion! I clearly felt the energy of a man. As he was making himself known to me, I felt... trapped. I don't know how else to explain it. He wanted me to feel limited. And there were two women there as well. I could here them arguing. One of them seemed very confused to as to whether you were the 'old mister.' I think it was the young woman who was killed in the pantry."

"You mean raped and killed." Nick sat down on the stool in front of his wife's vanity. He ran his hand through his hair as if trying to coax his brain to make sense of this.

"Yes. Raped and then killed. By the owner of the house; the man she called mister."

"Dear God. This woman thinks I raped her? Is she taking it out on Julianne? How do I convince a dead woman that I am not the guy who killed her?" Nick's voice was rising and he was shaking his head as if in utter amazement.

"Listen, Mr. Sullivan, I think you need more information. I think you need to contact PRISM, Paranormal Research and Investigative Society of Missouri. They use very technical methods to investigate and document hauntings. I have heard that they have been able to help other people in your situation."

"More strangers in my home?" Nick's voice was sounding shallow and his face was pale and slack.

"I know it feels like your home has already been invaded by strangers. My guess, these spirits feel the same about you. I would really recommend you try to do something. Your wife is sensitive to the stress and emotion in this house because she is pregnant. It sounds to me like that is complicating a pre-existing condition."

"You don't think the spirits here are deliberately trying to harm the babies?"

"No but I think they want you to leave and in trying they may end up hurting Julianne or you or the twins."

"I didn't tell you she was having twins did I?"

Savana smiled and patted his knee. "Listen, Julianne is likely to become less sensitive once the twins are born but the babies will be very sensitive to it. That kind of stress so early in life can affect the children's epigenetics."

"Epi what?"

"Epigenetics… It's kinda like the software that tells your genes to turn on or off. That software is constantly being written and rewritten through out your life. Very basic genes begin to express when we are very young. When a child is exposed to high stress really young, it can increase the child's chances of having mental illness, heart disease, cancer, diabetes and probably a slew of other things they haven't discovered yet."

"Wow. I hadn't heard of that."

"It's a fairly new area of research, and just now starting to make real headway. My point is, you do not want to bring the twins home to this kind of energy."

"What do I do?" He was looking ten years older than when they met in the drive less than an hour before.

"Call PRISM. See if they can help. If I were you, I would do everything I could to reclaim my home. And if that doesn't work, I would move."

As they walked out of the master bedroom, Savana glanced across the hall to the bedroom by the stairs. She had another small flash, this time of a young boy, looking rather sad as he had been banished to his room without supper. He was sitting on the frameless bed, staring at his dangling feet, arms crossed sternly across his slumping chest.

It was the oddest thing. Young Tommy looked up as she and Nick entered the hall and she thought for a moment that he was not a vision but had indeed manifested right there before their very eyes. Just as she was turning to ask Nick if he was seeing what she was seeing, she spotted something else. The sound that caught Tom's attention was the nearly inaudible giggle emitted from a slender nanny who was peering around the corner and into the room.

The 7-year-old Tom was looking uncertainly at her as she stood grinning her big tooth grin, the curls of her salt and pepper hair peaking out from beneath her cap. She gave him a little wave, and Tom deciding she must be real, waved back with a half-hearted smile. What he couldn't see was that at the bottom of her long gray skirts, just passed the cream stockings that her ankles wore, down where the tops of her old fashioned boots should have led down to solid soles on solid ground, there was nothing.

As fast as the scene had flashed to her, Savana blinked and it was gone. She smiled at Nick and continued past the room and down the grand stairs. She made a concerted effort not to see the hallowed faces staring out at her from the reflective surfaces throughout the house. She was emotionally drained. The house had definitely lived up to the reputation. Years of sadness and terror, energy so thick it seeped into the porous fabric of the house itself.

The wood of the floors, the glass in the mirrors, the material of the hundred- year-old drapes that still hung in the windows. Anything and everything that once had energy of its own had been steeped in the energy of the events that had plagued this house. So many sad souls, so much poverty and abuse. It was really the most disturbing place she had ever been.

As they traveled down the stairs Savana caressed the banister as they went. She had brief visions of children playing and one disturbing image of a bird hitting the plate glass window. When they got to the bottom of the stairs she had another vision from a much earlier time.

A young man stood arguing with his father in the great hall. He was visibly shaking and quite upset by whatever news his father had just given him. He grabbed the pin that was attached to the cravat that he had around his neck.

"To hell with you! To hell with the lot of you! You think I need your money but I don't. You marry your whore, you don't worry about me disturbing your wedding. You will never see me again!" With that he ripped the silver pin from the silk and hurled it at his father. He stormed from the house, slamming the door behind him.

Just one more family disturbed by the turmoil. Savana shook her head.

"I can't tell you if the energy that I feel is from the ghosts or the house itself. It seems to pulse with negativity."

"Is there anything else I can do besides call the paranormal group?

"Get the house blessed by a priest. Also, burning sage has helped in certain circumstances."

"Thank you for your insight and advise." Nick said genuinely grateful.

"Oh, and if you decide to tell your wife what is going on here, I would be happy to discuss with her what I have been seeing and feeling here."

"Thank you. I may take you up on that but I cannot tell her before the twins are born. We got to get through that hurdle first.

"Yes, I understand and agree with you. If she is safe and out of the house for now, use the time to try to fix this space. I wish you the best of luck." With a warm sympathetic smile Savana opened the door and walked out.

A few minutes later, Nick sat at his computer, shaming himself internally for ordering two sage smudge sticks to use in the house. How very open minded he had become.

Chapter Fifteen

Jordan Hawkes read the e-mail he'd received from Nick Sullivan first thing that morning. He reads and re-reads the claims of activity, and the history of the St. Joseph man's new home. The house was definitely old but in his experience, old did not mean haunted. In fact, he and his team believed that eighty percent of all events labeled as paranormal, really had perfectly logical explanations.

He was not however, a skeptic. His own paranormal experiences were what had driven him to seek out others who had experienced similar events. Through his website, he met a gentleman by the name of Gregg Watts. Gregg had experiences when he was a child that left him searching for answers all his life. With a lot of research and ingenuity they put together a team of investigators with various skills they felt would be useful in their quest for answers.

Over time they had perfected a process that was heavy on the science and wrought with electronic gadgets. The team would go into a location, set up digital recorders and cameras in all the areas in which "unexplained" events had previously occurred.

A team of six investigators would split up and move through out the home or business where the activity was happening. They would take along various pieces of hand held equipment. Things such as EMF or Electromagnetic Field detectors, which some say can detect the magnetic disturbances caused by paranormal entities that are attempting to manifest themselves into a physical form.

This was often accompanied by changes in temperature in the room or on surfaces where the activity happens. The team was equipped with a thermal recorder that could measure these changes.

Often times, the activity happened in areas without stationary cameras. Experience has taught them to carry mini digital video recorders to capture any activity they might encounter on their rounds.

Jordan and Gregg both had experience in home renovation. They had thirty years of combined experience with plumbing, electrical and carpentry work. They hadn't realized at the onset how valuable that knowledge would be in their new venture.

They were able to find loose fitting pipes that were creating the illusion of footsteps through hallways and in attics or basements. Using the EMF detectors, they were able to find exposed wires that were emitting unusually high readings. There was nothing like the relief on the face of a client when they explained how high EMF fields caused paranoia, nausea and an uncanny feeling of being watched. People who had extreme sensitivity to EMF fields could also experience delusions and hallucinations. So many "hauntings" could be attributed to faulty contracting.

Many could also be attributed to easily spooked people moving into old, scary looking homes, and freaking themselves out over the unfamiliar but otherwise normal bumps in the night.

Something about the tone of Mr. Sullivan's e-mail was different. It rang with the sound of desperation and an undertone of disbelief. In addition to that, it was clear that the man sought their help out of fear for his pregnant wife. As a father of five, the email struck a cord for Jordan.

He wanted to help this man get some answers. Maybe help him stake claim to his new home if they could. He flipped open his cell phone and called Deanna. She handled the majority of the administrative work for PRISM and he wanted her to get started on the logistics right away.

On the second ring, she answered, "Hey J, what's up?"

"How soon can you get to the office?"

"Got a live one?" The excitement in her voice was obvious.

"Oh yeah. I think we have the real deal. I want to get started on the history of the place right away."

"You got it, I am on my way there."

She was already on the road and with a quick left turn and she was headed toward headquarters. "So what's the case?"

"A couple in St. Joseph just moved into a house built sometime in the mid nineteenth century. They started experiencing activity as soon as they moved in and now, his wife, who is pregnant with twins has gotten sick, and the husband is afraid it has something to do with the spirits in the house."

"Whoa! Is he freaked?"

"Yes, completely. He really needs our help and soon. I would like to see if we can get a team together this weekend."

"Yeah, you got it. I will get on the phone with the guys as soon as we hang up."

"Thanks Deanna."

"No problem."

"I will call Gregg and fill him in on the details. Keep us informed."

"Absolutely. I'll call you back in about an hour."

After hanging up with Deanna, Jordan turned back to his computer and clicked the reply button on his e-mail. He wanted to let Mr.

Sullivan know right away, that he didn't have to deal with this on his own anymore.

"Oh man..." he said aloud to his empty office, "I sure hope we can help this guy."

Chapter Sixteen

Nick smiled at Julianne as she opened her eyes Friday evening. He had arrived forty five minutes earlier, a large bouquet of white roses in tow but she had been asleep when he arrived. He considered waking her but decided that the longer she slept the better. Not only for her but for him too. He had never hidden anything from his wife before and he was afraid she would see it as soon as she looked at his face.

He had wanted to tell her what he was doing but had ultimately decided it was a bad idea. She had been extremely frightened by the idea of ghosts in the house and he did not want to cause her any stress. The doctors had been very clear about that. In order to avoid creating a complication that would require taking the twins early and performing open-heart surgery on Julianne, she must remain calm.

So when she woke and smiled lovingly at him, he smiled back, even though inside he was a jumble of nervous energy and fear. Fear for his wife, his children. Fear for his sanity.

He must have flip-flopped a hundred times since he received the e-mail from Jordan Hawkes that morning. He kept going back and forth between being anxious to get answers from the paranormal team, and thinking his cheese had slipped off his cracker. *Ghosts? Really?*

He couldn't believe he was even thinking about it, but how else could he explain it? He looked down at his sleepy, smiling wife and decided he would think about it later. He needed to focus on Julianne right now.

"How are you feeling?" He asked.

"Tired. Thirsty."

Nick stood to fill her plastic pink cup from the plastic pink pitcher of water that sat on the table next to her bed. He was so relieved to have a distraction; he popped up off his stool a little too quickly and sent it clattering noisily across the floor.

"Nick." Julianne's voice was calm but firm.

He turned and looked at her, sure that his odd demeanor had made her realize he was hiding something.

"Honey," she said holding her hand out for his.

"Yeah babe?" He asked, taking it.

"I am going to be okay. I can feel it in my soul. I am going to be fine and so are the twins, okay?"

He realized at once that she mistook his guilt for concern. It made him feel even guiltier but he couldn't tell her the truth without risking her health so he went with the lie.

"I can't help but to worry. You're my whole life, the three of you. But don't you concern yourself over me. I'm the dad and it is my job to worry okay? I am fine, and I know you are all going to be fine too."

He leaned down and kissed her forehead, still avoiding eye contact. He turned away to get the water. He closed his eyes and took a deep breath before he turned and handed her the cup with the bendable straw in it.

She took it gladly and drank deeply until she had emptied the water from it. She handed the cup back to Nick, nodding when he asked if she would like another. Sipping it more slowly, she asked Nick questions about the house.

"Have the police been back out?"

"No."

"Well, has anyone broken in since the last time?"

"No. I think the cops showing up probably scared them away."

"Well that's a relief." She shifted in the bed, raising her self up to a better sitting position.

Nick didn't want to talk about the "intruder." He looked around for a way to change the subject. His eyes flitted across the bathroom and then back to his wife.

"I have been working on the bathroom." He smiled proudly.

At least that wasn't a lie; he had worked at a relentless pace all day. He was uncomfortable in the house but less comfortable leaving the dogs in there alone so he stayed. He told himself he worked at that pace so the bathroom would be finished when Julianne was able to come home. In the back of his mind, he knew that he was really just trying to stay busy. He figured if he stayed distracted, he wouldn't notice the odd things that were going on around him.

"Great! I have a feeling I am going to want to soak in that huge tub a time or two in the near future." She smiled at him playfully.

"Yeah, I am sure." Then Nick realized why the silly-grin.

"Wait a minute! How do you know what size the tub is? You've been peeking at my designs haven't you!"

"Busted!" She said with an enormous grin.

They both cracked up laughing. It was a good outlet for the pent-up anxiety Nick was feeling. His wife's laughter was one of his favorite sounds. He could almost forget about all the difficulties they were facing while listening to that laugh. But soon enough, the laughter died down and the nurse nudged open the door and reminded them that visiting hours were over.

"Well babe... guess I better go let the dogs out. Do you need anything the next time I come?"

"No. Thank you for the roses," she nodded at the flowers that he had set in the spare pitcher on the cabinet at the foot of her bed.

"Lovelies for my lovely." He kissed her on the mouth.

"I love you too."

Nick glanced at his watch as the elevator slid silently down to the bottom floor. He had an hour to go before the team of researchers from the paranormal association arrived at the house. Apparently he could expect six of them. They would need a quiet room to set up their monitoring station, and they would be running wires through out the house. The email told him to expect them to be there all night. He was welcome to stay and watch but they would like him to make other arrangements for the dogs.

He rented a room for the evening and had dropped them off before he went to see Julianne. He felt better about having them out of the house over night but did not relish the idea of going back to the house alone. He needed to kill some time so he headed to the library behind the mall.

He stopped at the desk to get a user name and password so he could access the Internet while he waited. He sat at a desk that was off somewhat by itself and pulled up the PRISM website again. He had seen earlier that he could read about the experiences other people have had. It was the best way that he could think of to feel better about his situation and maybe get a better idea of what to expect that night.

He saw pictures and read stories about other families who had experiences in their homes. There were even testimonials about how this particular team had helped them rid their homes of the ghosts that haunted them. Others felt they could make peace with the haunting, once they understood it.

In one respect it made Nick feel less crazy about what he believed was going on in his house. On the other hand, there weren't any stories about pregnant women getting hurt or sick. It felt like he was playing in a different ballpark from the stories he read.

One common thread in the stories was the fact that the activity seemed to increase when the paranormal team investigated. He saw pictures of scratches and swollen ankles as a result of "unexplained activity" according to the web site.

It went against his grain to leave strangers alone in his home but he really didn't want to be there if the activity escalated. He seemed to be a target for at least one of the ghosts. *No big deal, just the one who thinks I raped her.* He couldn't help feeling offended, even if she was a ghost.

He made up his mind and called Jordan Hawkes. The team had the run of the place, he and the dogs and going to stay at the hotel for the night.

Chapter Seventeen

The Prism van skidded to a halt in the gravel driveway of the old house. "War Pigs" by Black Sabbath blared from the open windows. Without turning off the music, a slightly soft, thirty something by the name of Miles Hoffstetter, AKA Hoff slid down from the driver's seat.

To look at him, one would assume he was a rock and roll hipster getting a little too old for his tattoos. His side burns were long, still evenly brown but his receding hairline gave his age away. He was a decent looking guy, if a bit pudgy and was described by all that knew him as a real stand up character.

He paused for a moment to hike up his loosely fitted jeans and straightened the hem of his "Disturbed" tee shirt. He slammed the heavy driver's door and loped to the back of the van. He was propping the doors open as the black SUV carrying his two bosses, Gregg and Jordan and the other two members of their investigative team.

The first was a young 22-year-old woman who had just joined the team. Her name was Maggie and her specialty was in using ultra violet video to record energy and heat. She could point her camera at anyone and with a few adjustments, she could measure the energy being exuded from their body. Some said that it looked as though she was capturing the aura of the subject.

The second team member was Ian, 30-years old and the manager at a local call center, his special skill was using EMF detectors in order to catch electromagnetic fields of energy. Usually, his equipment was good for finding bad wiring in a house, but occasionally he detected some unusual variations without any obvious source. The team used the information to focus their efforts in those areas.

Maggie was the first to exit the SUV. Her reddish blond hair, curly and long, bounced prettily around her face. She smiled a smile at Hoff and sauntered over to the van.

"Hey Hoff! You ready for tonight?" Her grin was indicative of her own excitement.

"You bet. Sounds like we got a real live one here."

"I heard that the psychic who visited the house said it was one of the most active places she had ever been." Maggie waggled her eyebrows to punctuate her statement.

"Really? Who was it, do you know?" he asked.

"Savana Williams."

"No shit? Wow, she is the real deal I think. We have been a couple of places that she has been and when she says there is activity, we usually have a boon of evidence by the end of the night. This could be good!"

"Yeah, I know. Jordan and Gregg were talking about the place as we drove. The history of the house is pretty amazing. Not a long list of owners, the original owner, the one the house was built for, died in the house. Then it was sold to a family that passed it down for three generations until the last of that family died in a freak accident in the shed at the back of the property. He was the third person to die on the property; the second was a nanny who died of a heart attack in the nursery.

When the last owner died, the city took the house for back taxes. They eventually sold it to an older woman who rented it out to a family in the 70's with six kids. By then the area was beginning to get really run down. The mother ended up dying of cancer, though not in the house, and the kids moved to Colorado to be with their father.

But before they went, they wreaked havoc in the neighborhood and convinced everyone it was haunted. The rumors stuck and the house remained empty. Again, when the old woman died, the property was seized for back taxes and until now no one has wanted to touch the place."

Hoff looked impressed with the information. He wanted to know more but when he opened his mouth to ask, he was interrupted by the long bellow of his own name.

"HOOOOFF!" Ian shouted as he exited the SUV. "Old man look at you! How long has it been?"

"Since the house on Penn Street I think." Hoff replied giving Ian a hardy handshake.

"I think so. I wish I could give up the call center and do this full time with you but you know...."

"Kids." they said in unison.

"Yeah." Ian chuckled. "So how are you? How is A-Lese?"

A-Lese was Hoff's girlfriend and sometime companion on the nights he investigated. Ian liked her in particular because she was a laugher. He could tell her any corny joke and she would just laugh and laugh. Plus she made the most delicious homemade fudge.

"Oh, she is good. She is working day shift now so she is gonna stay home and sleep tonight. But she did send some fudge." Miles smiled knowing the other man's affinity.

"Peanut butter?"

"And cherry walnut."

"Oh man! That is a good woman you got there! You should marry her before someone steals her away."

"I know I know. Jeez, you sound like my mother."

Ian laughed and picked up two of the many black cases from the back of the van. "Where are we setting up?"

Jordan answered as he and Gregg joined the group. "The dining room is going to be the command center. Hoff turn off that music it is almost ten o'clock."

Gregg stated that he would check in with the homeowner and the others began pulling boxes and wires out of the van to carry into the house.

Jordan leaned in close and whispered to his crew. "Listen up, Gregg is having some trouble at home. He is in a bit of a mood tonight, so don't anybody fuck up too bad OK?"

They all nodded in agreement. They were familiar with Gregg's mood swings but definitely appreciated the heads up. With knowing looks, they glanced at each other and Ian pointed at Maggie and said, "He means you!"

"Ha Ha." Maggie smiled back at him.

Maggie liked Ian. He was a genuinely good guy. He loved his kids and made nice with their mother even though their split was pretty nasty in the beginning.

He wasn't bad looking either, she had a thing for guys in glasses. She looked him over as he piled cases in sections to help make set up easier. He was wearing rolls of masking tape on his arm like bracelets. At 6'2" he was the tallest of the group and was designated to tape wires in high places if need be.

Maggie on the other hand was short. Only 5' so she always wore heals. The guys could never understand that her feet were used to them and did not hurt. She'd donned her first pair at 16 and had not looked back.

Tonight, she was wearing boots. Tall boots that came up to her knees. Her new, dark blue skinny jeans were tucked inside. She wore her curly hair in a pony tail that draped halfway down her back with a few curly strands left loose to frame her face. Ever the girlie girl, she wore several pieces of sterling silver jewelry on her neck and ears.

Ian of course wore plaid. He *always* wore plaid. *It's the Irish in him* she mused. They were both from big Irish families and she couldn't help thinking that her folks would approve.

The other three were dressed in their usual black hoodies and jeans. Their part of the investigation would undoubtedly be more physical than her own would be. They often had to crawl around in attics and crawl spaces under houses in order to find the source of mysterious noises. She on the other hand had merely to point and shoot. And keep her batteries charged. Her equipment would do the rest for her.

She was just stuffing her extra batteries into her camera bag when Gregg, the oldest of the group at 43 got back to the van.

"Okay, bring the stuff in through the carport door. Exit the kitchen to the south and head into the first room on the right. It's the dining room and you have permission to use the table for the monitors. Let's go. Chop. Chop."

His mood was showing.

Hoff gave Ian a look as he grabbed a couple of cases and handed them to Maggie. He grabbed a couple for himself and they headed off in the direction Gregg had gone.

As they entered the kitchen through the carport door, they could feel a chill coming from the house. Maggie thought that perhaps the heat was off. She would ask if they could turn it on for the investigation. If it were too hot or too cold in an environment, it would interfere with her equipment.

They deposited their gear in the library and followed Gregg on a tour of the old mansion. Even Hoff, who was not typically impressed by architecture, found the house impressive.

Each spot on the tour, where the homeowners had reported unusual activity, they put tape on the carpet or floor. This would help them later when they were focusing the six night vision cameras. They wanted to capture as much of those areas as they could with each camera.

By the time they were finished with the tour, there were around 12 'x' on the floor one in almost every room.

It would be a challenge to video a house of this size even with each team carrying an additional video camera as they investigated. So often, things happened in remote areas while the team was not there. Hopefully the static cameras would catch it and they would find it later when they reviewed the tapes.

The rooms that did not have an 'x' but were close to where activity was reported, would be equipped with sound activated voice recorders that would be left on throughout the investigation. With the plan in place, they began uncurling wires and hooking up monitors.

Chapter Eighteen

After two hours, the house was fully wired for video and sound. Gregg had not overseen much of it as he had toured the house with the owner and left the supervisory tasks to Jordan. He hoped everything would work well tonight. He had a feeling it would be an eventful night, and he wanted to be sure they captured that evidence on tape.

He had been surprised and fascinated by the house. One of the upstairs bedrooms had a secret passage leading from the closet, behind the pantries that lined the hallway, and exited a hidden door into the stair well of the attic. He was looking forward to spending some investigative time in the passage.

There was another secret room in the attic. It was a swinging wall attached at the top with piano hinges. The only way to get into the room was to push the bottom of the wall in until there was enough room to crawl beneath it into the small room behind. He made a mental note to have Maggie and Hoff do some EVP work in there.

EVP stood for Electronic Voice Phenomenon. It was rare but they sometimes could catch snippets of voices and sounds on tape that could not be heard by the investigators at the time they were recorded. They believed that sometimes these voices and sounds were paranormal.

They sometimes caught images with their infrared and thermal imaging cameras. Gregg had seen some pretty remarkable evidence of apparitions in his time. He knew that there were spirits that got trapped on earth after death. He had seen too much to doubt it.

However, every single investigation he did, he started off skeptical. Most of the time they were disappointed by the ease with which they discounted the events in the home by puzzling out exactly what the cause was.

It was the two investigations out of ten that yielded evidence of the paranormal (and by proxy his own sanity) that kept him working in this field. It certainly wasn't the money! With the cost of the equipment and travel, his association barely broke even.

Luckily, with the exception of Deanna who did full time administration for the group, the employees of PRISM were volunteers. Each of them had their own reasons for wanting proof of the paranormal. Most had experiences of one type or another in their own lives.

Gregg had seen the vision of his grandmother after she died. A soldier whose picture he had received during a pen pal exchange at school haunted Jordan. Maggie wanted to know if her deceased mother was on the other side and Hoff just liked anything that would scare him.

Ian's tale was a bit different. He was on a spiritual journey. Always looking for proof that the soul moves on. He never admitted to the group that his fear was that we did not go on and he would never know life after death. He wanted very much to see how things turned out for his kids and some day, his grand kids.

The last member of the team, who's gray Toyota was pulling into the drive was Deanna. Deanna was not just the administrator of the group but she was also a bit of a psychic. She could sense things before they happened and was a corner stone of their team. She could walk into a residence and feel which rooms were more likely to produce evidence. For all of them, evidence was the key.

Deanna did not have any technical talent and therefore did not come early enough to help set up. She liked to wait until the team could focus on what she was feeling and saying before she arrived on scene. The others did not mind, especially because she brought coffee and donuts when she did arrive.

Balancing her bounty with one hand, coffee tray in her grip and the bag of donuts around her arm, she knocked lightly on the front door.

Jordan had been waiting for her arrival. He really needed coffee to help deal with his partner's moodiness. Even so, he barely heard the knock on the door. He put down the extra wires he had been returning to their cases and trotted down the hall.

When he pulled the door open, a wave of energy smacked Deanna square in the chest and she almost dropped the coffee. Jordan was torn between grabbing the coffee and grabbing Deanna. She looked as though she might fall over.

"What's wrong?" he asked, alarmed. He had decided to steady her elbow that held the coffee in an effort to keep both the woman and her load from hitting the dirt.

"Whoa. Nothing really, just major energy here. I have never felt anything like it. It's as if the house screamed at me as you opened the door."

Seeing that she was again steady on her feet, he grabbed the coffee and led her down the hall to the dining room. The others jumped to as he walked in, ready to grab a cup.

"Hey y'all." Deanna said absently setting the bag of donuts on the table.

"Are you all set up and ready to turn out the lights?" She asked.

Turning out the lights was an important part of their investigation. Not only did it remove Electro-magnetic fields, or EMF's from registering off running fixtures but it also removed distractions, such as photographs and bric-a-brac, for the team. It was easy to find oneself focusing on the personal effects of the houses inhabitants, and therefore being unfocused if something paranormal did happen. Often the activity was subtle.

"Yeah," Jordan said. "We are ready to go. You got a feeling of where we should start first?"

"Well, yes and no. It feels like anything could happen hear. So much energy, I can't say for sure which room is worse."

"Well, then let's split up and do some EVP work and see if we can catch any voices." Jordan said. "Deanna you and Gregg start down here in the kitchen. See if you can recreate the blue light incident. Maggie, you and Hoff start up stairs. Ian and I will take the first watch on the monitors. We will let you know if the camera's catch anything you should investigate."

Everyone nodded their agreement and went off in separate directions. Jordan plopped into a seat and stirred his coffee. After a few minutes, he was about to grab a donut when he noticed something odd on the monitor in front of him.

Grabbing a walkie-talkie, he punched the button and said," Maggie, you guys aren't in the attic yet, right?"

"No, not yet, just checking out the first of the bedrooms. Why?"

"Well, there seems to be some sort of vibration happening in the attic. Do you guys hear anything?"

"No, nothing. Should we go check it out? What is it that you see?" Hoff asked through his own walkie-talkie.

"There is an old dress form up there and it looks like its jumping around a bit. Check it out. It's probably a vibration from an air conditioner or something."

"You got it, on our way up the stairs now. Careful if you guys come up this way, the bottom steps are missing."

"Missing? Can you get around them? If it is too dangerous don't do it. I don't want anyone getting hurt. Like I said, probably a vibration anyway."

Maggie looked at Hoff and he shrugged. "Let's check it out."

They looked back at the toy box they had discovered in the bedroom closet. Hoff wanted to look at it more closely when they had the opportunity. Something about it gave him the creeps and he loved to be creeped out.

Chapter Nineteen

Maggie was the first to top the stairs to the attic. She shone her light around the room until it found the dress form Jordan was talking about. It was not moving at all.

"Hey Jordan, it's pretty still up here now. Does it still look like its moving on the video?" Hoff said as he peered over Maggie's shoulder.

"No and it was kind of odd timing. It stopped jumping as soon as your flashlight hit the top stairs. Check the night vision camera to be sure it's taped down tightly and then check the mannequin to see if it is wobbly."

Miles crossed the room to the dress form and put his hand on the shoulder. A light blue spark accompanied the shock he felt as he made contact.

"Damn, shocked myself," he laughed.

"Does it wobble?" Maggie asked.

"Nope, steady as can be and heavy. It would take a hell of a vibration to knock it around." He relayed the message to Jordan.

"Why don't you guys do some EVP up there? See if we catch anything."

"You got it boss." Miles replied.

Both he and Maggie had voice recorders with them and they switched them on. Maggie, being the newest member of the group still felt shy about talking to the darkness so she motioned for Hoff to go ahead.

"Okay, EVP session one with Maggie and Miles here in the attic. Is there anyone else up here with us?" He asked in a loud clear voice.

"Anyone who want's to make contact with us? Now is your chance. Can you give us a sign that you are here?" He continued.

Just as the words left his mouth a large bang came from the back room of the large two-room attic.

"What was that?" Maggie asked.

"Maybe that was our sign." Miles answered as he moved toward the source of the sound.

"Careful, watch your step Miles."

Miles grinned. She was worried about him. She had a point however, since the stairs were falling out, who knew what kind of shape the attic floor was in. He slowed his pace and began testing the floor as he went. It was surprisingly solid and didn't even squeak.

As he rounded the corner to the second room, Maggie was hot on his heals. Her eyes were a bit wide and Miles could tell she was creeped out by more than the condition of the floor.

He shined his flashlight around the room and saw boxes stacked floor to ceiling. The cardboard was old and starting to sag from the humidity. Nothing seemed out of place. Lifting his recorder to his mouth, he began with a new tactic. He wanted to be antagonistic toward anything that might be here. It often produced better EVP's if he did.

"What, is that all you can do? That was pretty lame. You want to scare the poor pregnant lady who lives here? What kind of scary spirit are you supposed to be?"

At first, it didn't seem as though anything would happen but then Maggie yelped and moved closer to Miles.

"What?" he asked.

"I think something touched me. It felt, I don't know, like a hand being set on the top of my head maybe. It was super weird!"

"Oh, sure you like picking on women don't you? Are you a man or a woman? Are you a bully who just likes to touch the females? Why don't you try something like that with me, huh?" Miles practically shouted.

Just then, a sound came from the other room. It sounded like a scrapping sound, or maybe a rolling chair moving fast across the floor.

"Whoa! You guys get back into the other room! The mannequin is moving! Is it on wheels?" Ian asked from the radio.

Miles, slightly in front and ahead of Maggie quickly jogged back into the other room, disregarding the possible issues with the floor. The beam of his flashlight caught site of the mannequin as it came flying across the floor. It wobbled back and forth as though it was trying to walk toward them.

Miles jumped back and banged into Maggie who yelped and fell backwards into the second room. Miles could see the dress form was heading right for her. He had no time to think so as the form got close enough, he hauled off and punched it. It stopped in its tracks but did not fall over.

"Okay, so maybe antagonizing it was not the best idea," he said as he helped Maggie to her feet.

"I can't believe that just happened. Hey Jordan, Ian did you guys see that on the monitor?" He was hoping so, as it would be pretty fantastic evidence.

"Partially, we got it rolling toward you but it goes off camera. What happened when it got to you?"

"Well, I punched it. I couldn't think of any other way to stop it from running over Maggie and this damn thing is heavy! By the way, no wheels, it WOBBLED its way across the floor!"

"What? No way!" Ian exclaimed into the handset. "Mags are you hurt?"

"Just a little. I seamed to have scratched my side when I fell."

Why don't you guys finish up in the attic? Ask a few general questions and then call it." Jordan said.

"You got it boss, but I think another team should come this way before the night is over."

Miles turned to Maggie and asked, "Are you okay to finish up?"

"Sure. Let's do it. Who pushed the mannequin? What is your name?"

Jumping right in Miles asked, "Why do you try to scare people? Do you want us to leave?"

Maggie continued," If you want us to leave give us another sign."

They both waited silently. Hoff spun in a slow circle shining his light across the attic. Nothing seemed any different than when they first entered, with the exception of the mannequin being on the other side of the room.

After a few tense moments, Hoff and Maggie decided that the energy in the attic had expelled itself with the dress form and so they headed toward the stairs.

Chapter Twenty

Deanna felt drawn to the pantry the moment she and Gregg entered the kitchen. They often got paired together because the combination of her ability and his skepticism made for a thorough investigation.

"I'll check the appliances for EMF leaks." Gregg said.

"Okay, I am going to do an EVP in the pantry. I get a strong pull toward there."

"Okay, well why don't I scan it first so we can be sure that it is not EMF's that you are feeling."

"Sure, okay go ahead." She sat down at the kitchen table to wait.

As soon as she touched the surface of the table she felt an enormous grief. Fear and regret were in there too. She closed her eyes and concentrated to see if she could get a sound or a picture in her head. Almost as soon as her eyes closed, a vision came storming in.

Deanna was not used to seeing a vision play out like a home movie and she was so started and out of her comfort zone she almost opened her eyes. She managed to hold them squeezed tightly shut and tried hard to listen to what was being said by the family that suddenly surrounded her at the table.

"Don't any of you tell mom what happened!" a brown-haired girl of about 13 said sternly to the other five children sitting at the table.

The oldest male rolled his eyes and said, "You don't tell us what to do Laurie!"

"Shut up Pat! You know we can't tell mom, we will all get in trouble." Said the oldest girl.

Deanna couldn't decide whether she was older than the boy called Pat, or if they were perhaps twins.

"Why would I get in trouble?" Asked the littlest boy, who was covered from head to toe in dirt.

"Because we were all there and we were all taking turns on the trapeze. And Pat you were the one driving the bike too fast when Laurie grabbed it. Its *your* fault that she broke her arm!" Huffed the blond girl.

"Shut up Lee, you don't tell me what to do either. I am only 10-months younger that you!" said Pat rather loudly.

With that the youngest girl, also blonde, also covered head to toe in dirt began to cry.

"Oh great!" said Lee.

"Pat, you asshole!" Said Laurie picking the toddler up with her good arm.

"It's okay Kimbo. Don't worry, I didn't break my arm, I just bent it a little. I will be okay and no one is going to tell mom!"

Lee turned to a scruffy red-haired boy and said "Danny go round up the dogs, it's time for them to eat."

With that the vision blinked out and another vision started. This time the film appeared to be set in the carport out front of the kitchen.

The same boy they called Pat was sitting on a motorbike and a very tall woman with an East Coast accent was yelling at him to just go!

"Go run off to your grandmother then! You're not welcome here anymore!" With that, the woman slammed the door and locked it. She waited until the motorcycle roared away before she slid down the door and collapsed into tears.

The overwhelming feeling that Deanna got was the feeling of having failed. This woman was obviously the children's mother and she was a likely source of the chaotic energy that remained in the house.

The image blinked out and Deanna was left with the blackness of her eyelids. She opened her eyes and blinked a couple of times. Gregg was standing at the end of the table staring at her quizzically.

"What was that?" He asked.

"I don't know. I..." She trailed off, not ready to share the extremely personal experience she had just had.

"I just feel a lot of sadness here. I think this house makes people sad." She almost whispered the last.

"Well, if it does, it isn't because of EMF. The pantry is clear if you want to do your EVP."

"Thanks."

She walked over and stood in the dark pantry with the door closed and her flashlight off. She asked the standard questions, who is here, what do you want us to know, how can we help you, etc...

She was just wrapping up when there was a loud scream followed by multiple thuds coming from just above the stairs to the kitchen.

Gregg was closer to the stair well and made it up first to find Maggie lying breathless at the bottom of the attic stairs. Hoff scrambled down after her, and slid across the plywood covering the last few stairs.

"Maggie! Are you hurt?" The men said almost in unison.

Maggie couldn't answer, the wind had been knocked out of her as she hit the floor and her knee was throbbing from taking the wait of her body when she first fell. *No. Not fell*. Maggie was certain she had been pushed.

When she was finally able to pull in a shaky breathe she said as much to the team who was by now all coming up the stairs.

"Okay, okay give her some room!" Jordan said.

The others stepped back and let him help Maggie into a sitting position. She winced as her legs straightened out. As she got to her feet she realized she could put pressure on it but her knee ached immensely. She leaned on Jordan and they made their way back down to the dining room command center.

"You gonna be okay? Do you want to go the ER?"

"No." She heard the shaking in her voice and said more firmly "No. This family needs our help."

"Why don't you take my spot at the monitors for now? I will head to the master bedroom with Hoff."

"Sure, okay but I don't want to sit out all night. I will be ready to go again as soon as my knee stops aching."

"IF your knee stops aching." Jordan said dryly.

He grabbed his equipment and headed back up stairs, passing Ian on the way.

"Hey Ian, just a second." He stopped halfway up the stairs and turned back to look at Ian.

"Make sure you two stay together, okay. Seems like this mission is doomed for her."

"I gotcha," Ian replied. "I got her back, no worries." He trotted the rest of the way to the control area.

Chapter Twenty-One

Jordan and Gregg were in the master bedroom, sitting in the dark on opposite sides of the bed. They were just waiting at this point to see if anything would happen.

"I guess I've been a bit of an ass today." Gregg said.

"You wanna talk about it?" Jordan asked. They had known each other for 10-years and were about as close as brothers.

"It's Nancy," he said referring to his wife. "She wants me to quit PRISM."

Jordan looked up sharply at the sound of his friend's words. He clicked on his flashlight to find Gregg holding his head in his hands.

"You can't be serious." Jordan stated.

"Yeah. She says we can't be a normal family if I run off over night every weekend."

"Doesn't she know how much this means to you?"

"Yes. She just wants her and the kids to mean more I suppose." Gregg gave a half-hearted smile.

"Maybe you could take a couple weekends off and see if she comes around."

"I don't know if a couple of weekends...."

Before Gregg could finish his sentence, the light flashed on overhead.

"What the..." Jordan said startled and somewhat blinded by the sudden illumination of the overhead light.

"Look!" Jordan pointed to the switch over by the door. It was in the off position.

"What could make that come on with the switch off?" Gregg asked.

"Quick, get your video on and let's start an EVP."

"Do you smell that?" Gregg asked.

After a moment Jordan did. "Yeah. Pipe smoke?"

"Yeah. Look at the light!"

Gregg looked up and the light was surrounded in a ring of smoke. It looked like someone had just blown it out of his or her mouth. He aimed the camera at it and watched on the display as the smoke dissipated.

For the sake of due diligence, Jordan called down to the other team members and asked them if anyone was smoking.

"No. The homeowner is still gone and no one on the team smokes. You know that."

"Yeah. Just had to check for sure."

He didn't mention the fact that it smelled like pipe or cigar smoke in hopes that the phenomenon would recreate itself for another team later in the night. This would provide confirmation if they described the smell the same way.

It was common practice with the team when they had personal experiences to withhold certain details from each other, not only to confirm the activity but also to keep from influencing the opinion of the rest of the team about the event.

"You get it on tape?" Jordan asked.

"Yeah, it looks like it." Gregg replied having rewound the hand held video camera far enough to watch the smoke dissipate again.

Switching on his voice recorder Jordan asked, "Who smokes a pipe?"

"Why do you want us to know you are here?" Gregg asked after a few seconds of silence that would hopefully give time for a response of some sort from an entity or spirit.

"Is someone trying to hurt the people who live here?" He continued.

"Are you trying to hurt the babies?" Jordan asked, and then decided to add "Why?"

After about twenty minutes of questions in this vein, they clicked off the recorders, and began to exit the room. Jordan flipped the light switch up and then back down. The lights went dark.

"Hmmm, could be faulty wiring." He said.

Gregg just looked at him and shook his head and said, "You know I don't like to say a place is haunted but I don' think that was a faulty switch."

They headed down to the command center to check in with the others. After a short consultation they reassigned teams including the limping Deanna, with the plans to cover the back yard, the basement and the secret passages.

By the time the sun started to rise, the team was both excited and exhausted. They felt certain they had more evidence on tape and video that they weren't even aware of yet. Deanna in particular was drained.

"That was both amazing and frightening!" She said.

Just as they were packing up the van with the last of the equipment, Nick Sullivan pulled into the driveway. The dogs were in the backseat, pacing and whining. Nick had a pinched look on his face. He stepped out of the car and walked the few feet to shake Jordan's outstretched hand.

"How did it go? " He asked.

""Well, we don't like to say one way or the other about paranormal activity until we see the entire scope of evidence on tape." It was a canned response he gave every client at the end of the investigation.

"When will you review the evidence?"

"Give us 24 hours. We need to get a few hours of sleep and then comb through all the video and audio we took. We want to be sure we document all of the evidence before we get back to you. So, why don't you plan to come to the office tomorrow morning around 10 AM. We will have coffee and bagels."

With that, Nick shook hands with each member of the team and thanked them for their efforts. He waited in the driveway until the three PRISM vehicles disappeared around the corner before he turned to look at the house.

It didn't feel as ominous in the day light. Still, he felt a sense of doom as he released the dogs from the car and made his way to the door.

Chapter Twenty-Two

After the first hour in the house without anything unexplained happening, Nick began to feel silly. The dogs even looked more comfortable as they lay at his feet in the library. He wanted to look through the books to see if he could find any amazing volumes to surprise Julianne with at the hospital.

He was trying hard to concentrate on the titles on the shelf in front of him but his attention kept getting pulled to the old map which was still lying open on the desk. He approached it slowly, almost as if he expected something to jump out of the map at him. He leaned over and traced the roads to the intersection where the house would be built two years later.

He was just about to look at the little cemetery next to their land when he heard a scraping noise coming from behind him.

He thought, *oh shit here we go.* He stood up slowly and listened before turning around. He heard it again. A soft scraping noise like a loud whisper of papers being scooted across a desk.

He glanced over at the dogs and both were looking intently at something behind and slightly above him. He felt his blood turn cold, and his hair stand up on the back of his neck. He was frozen in place. He wasn't sure what to do.

At the third occurrence of the scraping sound, Nick finally whipped around. His breath caught in his throat and his eyes took a moment to focus. He looked at the space between him and the door of the library. At first, he saw nothing unusual. He had been so scared that there would be someone standing behind him that his relief was palpable.

He started to chuckle, a nervous little sound that was a little crazy even to his own ears. The sound made him laugh harder. Before long, tears were running down his face and both dogs were standing in front of him wagging their tales and tilting their heads with curiosity.

"Daddy is a dolt." He said. Then he heard the sound again, this time a little higher up than before. He stopped laughing and stood up straight. That is when he noticed it.

The books. Every other book was pulled out, their spines even with the edge of the shelf. Every other book was pushed in all the way to the back of the shelf. As he watched, a number of books slid forward of their own volition. It both terrified and angered Nick.

"Oh okay, you want to play games. Well FUCK YOU! This is my house now. I never raped you or killed you... any of you!" He shouted loudly.

The dogs began to whimper and he turned to comfort them when he heard another, louder scraping sound. He turned his face toward the sound and was smacked dead in the mouth with a large hard cover volume from the shelf.

He was so stunned he did nothing but stand there and let his eyes water. Seconds after the first book hit him, it began to rain books down on him. He threw his arms up and called for the dogs and ran. He came close to falling, a couple of times, as paper missiles continued to pelt him, as he made his way to the door. He stumbled over books on the floor and practically fell out of the room with the dogs fast on his heals.

"That's it. Fuck this! Let's go guys. We are going for a ride."

They bounded out the front door and ran quickly to the car. He caught site of his neighbor across the street, watching him with her hand fluttering nervously at her throat. He considered talking to her but dismissed it immediately.

Whatever she knew would likely be rumor and might think he was crazy if she didn't believe the rumors. He leaned into the car and pulled the door shut behind him. He had no idea what he was going to do but he had to find a place for the dogs before going to see his wife. He couldn't leave them in the car.

He decided he would rent a hotel room again for the next few nights. At least until he got the information from PRISM he didn't feel right about leaving them alone in the house. Nor did he want to go back inside. Ever.

Chapter Twenty-Three

When Julianne saw the welt on his lip she immediately frowned. He looked as though he had been in a fight. Even his eye was starting to darken as though he would have a shiner in a matter of minutes.

"What happened?" She looked at him, her voice full of concern.

"I was working on the bathroom and a plank of wood fell over and caught be in the face." He lied.

"You have to be more careful! What if it had knocked you out? You really shouldn't do anymore work until I am there with you."

"Yeah, I came to the same conclusion." He smiled his best false smile at her.

"Yeah right. Well come over here and hug us, will you?"

He crossed over to the bed and leaned down to hug and kiss his wife. "How are all of you doing?"

"Well, the nurse made a slip. Do you want to know what we are having?" She grinned at him.

"Well yeah, I guess if you already know then I want to know too!" He hadn't really wanted to be surprised anyway. That was Julianne's idea.

"Well... let's just say the velveteen rabbits can stay" Her smile was broad and lovely.

"Girls? Both of them?" He stared at her in disbelief. "I thought we would get at least one boy."

"Are you disappointed?" She asked.

"No. I thought I would be but I am not. I have two little girls! Oh man. I have two little Julianne's. I am so screwed...." He laughed out loud.

"You are. They are going to wrap you around their tiny little fingers from the moment they are born!" Julianne laughed along with him.

"I know. I know." He smiled lovingly at his wife.

He couldn't imagine how he was going to tell her what was going on in the house. He decided not to tell her anything yet. He still had a few weeks to figure things out before she was due to deliver.

He put the house out of his mind and instead decided to enjoy his time with his family. He would have plenty of time to fix this before they came home.

Chapter Twenty-Four

Nick was lying back against the headboard in the Days Inn hotel room on Frederick Ave. It was a nice room, though it smelled vaguely of old smoke. It was the first place he found that would allow him to have his dogs. Even so, he had to give a little demonstration for the manager to put his mind at ease. He showed him how obedient the dogs were and explained how he had adopted them through a program in New York that helped retired police dogs find homes.

After a few minutes of heal, fetch and stay, the old Indian man seemed to relax about the dog's size. Nick couldn't blame him, the wrong dogs could do a lot of damage to a hotel in short order.

Atlas and Asia now occupied the second queen size bed in the room and between the two, they completely covered the bed. They were enjoying having all the space to themselves.

Nick was looking at the local news broadcast but he wasn't seeing what was on the TV. His mind was reliving the experience in the library. He kept feeling the books pelting him with such force. Whatever was in that house was very strong. How could he take his newborn daughters' home to that house? He couldn't. He knew that he just couldn't.

He sat up, shifting the box of half eaten pizza onto the floor. He went to the sink and pulled another Heineken from the ice he had dumped there. He twisted the beer and looked in the mirror.

Just as Julianne had expected, he was sporting a black eye. Also, he had a cracked and swollen lip and several smaller scratches on his neck and scalp. He looked like he had gotten his ass kicked. He shook his head. If they could do this to him, what could they do to two defenseless babies?

He had to fix this and he had to do it soon. He wanted to be sure the ghosts were gone before he let his family into the house.

He looked at his watch. It was 7 PM. He wondered if he could get in touch with any of the Catholic churches this time of night. Things sure seemed to close early in St. Joseph. Even on Saturday nights.

Nick was moving toward the phone book on the nightstand when his cell phone rang in his pocket. The loud sound in the otherwise quiet room made him jump. He grabbed the phone and took a deep breath to calm himself before answering it.

"Nick Sullivan."

"Nick, it's Jordan Hawkes. Is this a bad time?"

"No, not really. What's up? I wasn't expecting to talk to you until tomorrow morning."

"I know but listen, there is something I think you need to hear right away. Could you come down now?"

"Yeah sure. Where are you exactly?"

"On Francis between 6th and 7th street down town. Do you think you can find it?"

"Yeah. I can find that no problem. I will see you in ten minutes."

He hung up the phone and grabbed his car keys off the dresser. He closed up the pizza box and patted each dog on the head before heading out the door.

The PRISM office was a small storefront in the historic down town area. Beyond the small lobby was one big room full of folding tables and computer screens. Deanna directed him to sit at the long table at the far back of the room and said that Jordan would be right with him.

She went to the fridge in the front corner of the large room and retrieved him a bottle of Coke. He sat sipping it, looking at the blank computer, wondering just what it was that Jordan needed him to hear.

He didn't have to wait long. Jordan came through the front door within five minutes of Nick's arrival. He shook Nick's hand and sat to boot up the computer. *I wouldn't want to play poker with this guy,* Nick thought. Jordan's face held no clue as to what he was preparing to show Nick.

"Okay, first let me tell you that we all had some sort of personal experience that we could not explain while in your house. It was probably the most active house we have been in this year. Maybe ever."

Nick grimaced at the news. He knew already that it was haunted and he had suspected that it was bad. Hearing it from Jordan just made him feel worse.

"I take it you got some sort of evidence on tape then?" Nick asked.

"Yes, many pieces. On video and on the voice recorders. We normally would get some rest before scanning the recordings but we were all very excited to see what we had captured. We started combing through it as soon as we returned this morning. The others just left about 20 minutes ago to finally get sleep. I knew that I would not be able to sleep without having warned you of what we found." Jordan's face did not hold an ounce of humor in its expression.

"Warn me? Warn me of what?" Nick suspected he knew what was coming.

"Let me just play you the tapes and let you decide for yourself what you think."

He clicked the mouse and opened a folder called Messanie EVP. He turned up the volume on the speakers and clicked play.

The voices Nick heard first were that of Deanna and Ian noting that they were in the nursery. They began asking questions and at first there was no answer. Then Ian asked the question:

"Who are you? How many are you?"

The voice that came next was louder than the human voices. It was somehow more solid.

"Our house."

Then the question what is your name?

The voice answered "Henry"

"Are you trapped here?"

"Yes. We all are."

That was the first recording and the least spectacular as far as Jordan was concerned. He clicked on the next one but didn't play yet.

"The next piece is also in the nursery but it is a little later in the night with myself and Maggie."

Maggie's voice asked, "Why are you trying to hurt the people in this house?"

The voice that responded was female this time. It was a scratchy and angry sound. It said, "HE hurt ME!"

"What do you want from the people in this house?"

Ian's voice was interrupted on the tape by the angry voice " I will hurt them. ALL of them!"

Jordan was looking at Nick expectantly. He didn't make a move to play the recording again or move on to another.

"Is that it?" Nick asked.

"No offense Mr. Sullivan, but that is one of the clearest EVP's I have ever heard.

"I don't mean to discount it. I just wanted to know if there was more."

"Yes, quite a bit more; photos, video and audio. I just had to be sure you were aware that there is a clear threat here. We also talked to the neighbors this afternoon. They had quite a lot to say. Especially a woman named Phyllis who has lived across the street from the house for 40 years."

"What did she say?"

"Well, she has gotten to know three families who lived in the house. Each she found to be normal when they arrived. In each case, the families broke up and came to hate each other. Also, each of the three mothers who lived in the house became ill while living there. The last dying of cancer."

"Jesus. I can't believe it. It's the house, making them sick. I don't care how crazy that sounds but it can't be a coincidence."

"I agree, especially in light of all the evidence we gathered."

"What else?" Nick braced himself.

"First, take a look at these pictures." Jordan slid the 4x6 prints across to him.

Nick could see the torso of one of the female investigators. She was holding her shirt up showing a series of scratches just below the rib cage on her right side.

"This happened in the house?"

"Yes. It happened in the attic. At first, Maggie thought it happened when she fell."

"She fell?" Nick asked, nervous about her having injured herself in his house.

"Hazard of the job. We walk around in the dark. However, the circumstances surrounding this fall were unusual. Take a look"

He clicked again with his mouse and this time a black and white video began to play. Nick watched as the dress form wobbled across the floor seemingly of its own volition.

"Just as it gets off camera, one of our guys had to punch it to keep it from running over Maggie who fell when Miles bumped into her. The more disturbing incident happened off tape unfortunately.

"More disturbing than an old mannequin walking around by itself?"

"More disturbing to Maggie. She was shoved down the attic stairs as they ended their session. That is why there is no tape of it."

"Is she alright?" Nick asked.

"Twisted her ankle but she will be fine. She is more upset that they didn't have a recorder going at the time."

"I believe her, and you. Julianne almost fell through the stairs in that spot. I think now that was not the work of termites."

"That isn't all that happened in the way of personal experiences but the others are fairly benign. I myself witnessed smoke appearing and disappearing in the master bedroom. It was accompanied by the smell of pipe smoke. Here, I can show you that one, we got it on tape."

Jordan told him about the light coming on by its self and how the switch moved. He went on to explain that Deanna had felt and seen things about the last family that lived there, how their energy was still strong and so very sad.

"Another piece of interesting evidence we caught last night was this." Jordan clicked play on another of the videos.

"What am I looking for?" Nick asked as he recognized the third small bedroom.

"Watch the toy box in the closet."

It took several seconds for it to register that the toy box was moving. Jordan turned up the volume and Nick could hear a quiet steady creak from the wheels as it slowly moved itself out of the closet.

"Let me speed it up a little bit." Jordan clicked again.

As the video fast-forwarded, the toy box shot back and forth across the room. It moved itself several times throughout the six-hour investigation.

Jordan showed Nick a couple of other videos. In one, a bedroom door shut itself, slamming loudly. On another a colorful array of colors surrounding the kitchen table. As he watched, the colors, which indicated heat and energy remained steady until Deanna entered the frame. A color storm erupted on the screen. It was during the part where she had her vision Jordan explained.

There were also a couple of voice recordings that were not as complete as the first one but were clearly voices from beyond. They were almost through the last of them when Nick's phone rang.

"Nick Sullivan." He answered.

"Mr. Sullivan, my name is Abigail Kawlewski, I am a nurse at Mosaic Life care. There has been a change in your wife's condition. We are going to need to you to come as quickly as you can.

"I am on my way." Nick looked frantically at Jordan. "It's my wife, I have to go right now."

"I hope everything is alright. Here! Take this, it's a copy of the evidence." He handed Nick a thumb drive.

Nick nodded his thanks and then ran out of the building and to his car. He thundered down the streets to the highway and prayed he would not get pulled over.

Chapter Twenty-Five

Nick rushed through the automatic doors and up to the information desk. He gave his wife's name and a elderly woman in pink scrubs told him to follow her to the NICU.

"I am Abi, we spoke on the phone."

"What is the NICU?" He asked they briskly moved through the halls.

"The Neonatal Intensive Care Unit."

"Are the babies alright? Is my wife alright?" He asked her, a lump in his throat made the words come out in a rasp.

"Your wife is having a cesarean section after having a small episode with her heart. So far everyone is stable."

They arrived at a waiting area and his escort pointed to a chair. "Wait here for the doctor to bring you an update.

This," she said handing him a round plastic object with lights, "is a pager. Like the kind they give you at a restaurant. If you need to use the restroom or get a coffee, keep it with you.

If the doctor has information for you he will page you and the device will blink and vibrate. If you plan to go any farther than the coffee station, check in with the young lady at the desk." She pointed to a desk just down the tile hall from where he sat.

"Thank you. I will stay right here." Nick said feeling overwhelmed and light headed.

"Hang in there Mr. Sullivan. We are all rooting for you." Abigail said before rushing away back down the hall that had brought them there.

Nick stared at the door nurse Abi had indicated when she said the doctor would come update him. He wanted to rush through the doors and locate his wife but knew that he would just get in the way. He felt so helpless he wanted to scream.

It felt like an eternity before the doors opened and a doctor in surgical scrubs came through and called Nick's name.

"Here! Is my wife okay? The girls?"

"Your wife is fine but is going to need surgery. We are going to be taking her up in a few hours. The babies are stable but as you know are premature. They are being examined as we speak."

"Can I see Julianne?"

"Sure, right this way."

They walked down what felt like an endless corridor before turning to walk another endless corridor. Finally the doctor stopped and knocked lightly on room 2006. He waited a brief moment before pushing the door open and looking in. Apparently satisfied that Julianne was decent, he opened the door wider and permitted Nick to enter.

"Look who I found." Dr. Matthews said with a loud perky tone. "Don't get too worked up now, you hear? We don't want another episode before we get a chance to fix you up.

Go ahead and take about 15 minutes Mr. Sullivan, then if you could meet me at the nurse's station out the door and down the hall to the right."

Sure. Thank you doctor Matthews." He shook the older man's plump hand as he left the room.

"Jules!" Nick rushed immediately to his wife's side.

"They are too early." She whispered through a sob.

"I know babe. I'm scared too."

"I can't believe my heart betrayed me this way! I failed at my first task as a mother, I can't even keep them safe until they are ready to be born!" she wailed.

"Hey! Hey! Don't think that way. You have carried and kept them safe for almost eight months. They are going to make it. They are going to make it!" He said a second time a little more firmly.

He held Julianne while she cried. Eventually her soft even breathing told him that she had fallen asleep. He adjusted her back against her pillows and headed out to meet with the doctor.

"What happened?" Nick asked.

"Well, your wife's heart valve is narrowing at a fairly quick pace. Much quicker than we had expected and frankly faster than I have ever seen before. Her blood pressure became extremely high and we had no choice but to take the babies."

"Is she in danger?"

"Well, now that we have taken the babies, her body is no longer under such extreme stress, but we need to get a stint in place as quickly as we can. From there it will be a matter of after care but we will discuss that more fully before she is released."

"What should I do?" Nick asked, feeling lost and alone.

"Well, the surgery will take a few hours. You can see your daughter's in the meantime and we will page you if there is anything you need to know."

"My daughters!" Nick exclaimed as it dawned on him that they were here. No longer a vague dream but flesh and blood. His heart suddenly ached for them.

"Please, tell me where they are."

"Do ya one better. Myrtle here will be happy to walk you down there."

The oldest woman Nick had ever seen smiled up at him from between hunched shoulders. "Right this way honey."

They ambled slowly down the hall. Nick became impatient and considered briefly picking the old woman up, and carrying her down the hall but he resisted the urge.

Thankfully the room where the babies were being monitored was not far from where they had started. The girls lay side by side in matching incubators. Nick's heart skipped a beat when he saw the oxygen tubes attached to their tiny little faces.

Before limping slowly away, Myrtle helped Nick don a hospital robe over his clothing. He put on a hair-cap and slippers over his shoes. Once he was ready, Myrtle shook his hand and wished him good luck.

Nick entered the glass room through a glass door and looked around. There was an attractive black woman scribbling something on the chart that hung on the end of one of the incubators. She smiled at him and motioned toward the girls.

Nick moved slowly, feeling uncomfortable amongst so much medical equipment. His limbs were feeling numb and he was afraid he would stumble into something and break it. Instead he sank slowly into a rocking chair and leaned forward to look through the plastic at his daughters.

They were so tiny and their skin seemed a little transparent but to Nick they were the most beautiful babies he had ever seen.

He scanned their faces for signs of Julianne and himself. Their little pink lips were pursed but he could tell they would be full like his wife's. The rest of their faces were still too scrunched up to really be able to tell anything yet but he felt confident they had his eyebrows.

His heart was flopping around in his chest. He was falling in love with his daughters. He couldn't wait to hold them and coo at them. He wanted to teach them to play ball and work on cars, everything he would teach a son. No daughter of his would ever have to rely on a man.

He put his hands on the clear side of the plastic boxes that now held his heart. He marveled at their accomplishment and was humbled by their strength. They were survivors, just like him.

Chapter Twenty-Six

The surgery went smoothly. Julianne was stable and resting comfortably in the adult intensive care unit. Nick spent visiting hours with her, just watching her sleep. When visiting hours were over, he would go sit with his daughters, whose visitations were not restricted.

For the next several days, he spent as much time as he could at the hospital, without completely neglecting the dogs. He kept them at the Days Inn. He was uncertain as to what to do about the house. He knew he would have to go back soon, if for no other reason than to take in the mail. He didn't want to advertise that no one was currently staying there. Getting robbed at this point would be adding insult to injury.

Deciding on Wednesday that this would be the day, Nick took the short drive from the hospital to the house. As he approached the house from the east he noticed something odd. The outer set of double doors was propped open. It was not wide-open, just four or six inches.

"Christ, now what?" Nick said aloud to the empty car.

He hesitated for only a fraction of a second before exiting his vehicle and slowly approaching the front of the house. As he came around the corner he could see a small white box was tucked into the doors. FedEx! His smudge sticks, he had completely forgotten about them

Witchcraft! and Can't hurt!, echoed simultaneously through his thoughts. He was happy to have something proactive to do. He grabbed the box and entered the second set of doors with his key. His spine went stiff and his muscles bunched as the door swung open.

He took a couple of steps inside and stopped to listen. Silence greeted his straining ears. He looked around the grand hall and into the living room. Nothing moved with the exception of dust swirling in the rays of afternoon sun.

He looked at the package in his hands and wondered briefly if he was nuts. He had no idea how to use sage to clear a home but knew of someone who might. He just hoped she was available right away.

Savana Williams answered her phone on the third ring. She had been going through her paperwork trying to catch up on some much needed filing. She loved working for her self but found she lacked a certain discipline for mundane tasks. *Perhaps I will hire an assistant,* she thought as she reached for the phone.

"Hello?"

"Ms. Williams?"

"Yes, this is she."

"Nick Sullivan here."

"Oh, hello Mr. Sullivan, what can I do for you?"

"You can tell me that you're not too busy right now." He said hopefully.

"Well, I am working, just not with a client. What's going on? Something happening in your house?"

"No, not at the moment but I bought some sage you see and... I really don't know what to do with it. Could you come help me cleanse the house?"

"Oh! Well, there is nothing to it really. You could easily do it without my help. Just be sure you get smoke in every nook and cranny. Don't give them anywhere to hide from the smell."

"I will pay you double your fee to come walk through it with me right now." He stated this flatly but Savana could sense the desperation in his voice.

"Double huh? Well. I guess it's just paperwork, I can catch up later. I can be there in ten minutes. Fifteen if there is traffic on the Belt Highway." *Definitely need to get an assistant.*

"Thank you! Thank you so much!" Nick didn't realize how tense and uncomfortable he had been until the relief washed over him.

"One question Mr. Sullivan, why do you really want me to come help you?" Savana asked gently.

"So you can tell me if it works."

Ten minutes later, Nick had opened the sage bundles, gotten a lighter from the junk drawer and filled a couple of tumbler glasses full of water. He set everything together on the kitchen table and stepped outside to wait for Savana's arrival.

He didn't have to wait long before her silver Toyota was coming up the gravel drive. She exited the vehicle with papers in one hand and a 32-ounce fountain drink in the other. She smiled and lifted the glass in way of a salute.

"Hey, thanks for coming. I can't tell you how grateful I am."

Savana smiled and said, "You don't have to tell me Mr. Sullivan, I can feel it."

"Please call me Nick, can I help you with anything?" He motioned toward the stack of paper in her hand.

"Good Nick, please call me Savana. No thank you, I got this, it's just a few suggestions on what you might say as we walk through the house." She indicated the papers.

They went in through the carport door directly into the kitchen. Nick stopped short and Savana almost bumped him with her soda. He moved to the side and she could see the reason for his sudden anxiety.

The smudge-sticks, glasses, and lighter were on the floor. The glasses were shattered and the sage was soaking in the water.

"Shit!" Nick grabbed the bundles out of the puddle and began wiping them on his flannel shirt.

"I take it that is not where you left them." Savana said.

"No. They were on the table. Do you pick up on anything?"

"Yes. Anger. Fear. Loathing. I can't quite get where it's coming from though." She wrinkled her brow, unfamiliar and distressed by the unfocused energy.

"Should we start?" Nick asked.

"Yes, I think we should, here look these over and pick one you feel comfortable with." She handed him her stack of papers and then drew deeply on the straw in her soda.

While Nick looked through the blessings and proclamations, Savana examined the sage smudge sticks. Only one side had gotten wet and it didn't look like it had any real time to soak in. She felt confident that they would light.

Nick found an ownership proclamation that didn't make him feel ridiculous saying it. He quickly swept the broken glass into a wet pile by the door and grabbed two more tumblers from the cabinet by the sink. He put a little bit of water in the bottom of each one so they could safely extinguish the sage bundles when they were done.

They lit two of them and began moving about the large kitchen. While doing so, Nick proclaimed his ownership of the house by saying the phrase written on the paper.

"This in now MY home. I have bought and paid for it! I declare now, that any spirits, souls or energies that have the intention of harming the inhabitants of this house are not welcome here and must leave now!"

His voice grew bolder each time he said it. He repeated it in every corner of the kitchen. He looked at Savana to see if she was picking up on anything as they went.

"I do feel that the souls that are trapped here are moving away from the smoke." She said. "Let's move out into the hallway then hit the dining room, living and library. Then we will head upstairs."

"Good. Let's go"

Nick continued to make his proclamation every few minutes as they traced windows and doors with the sage's earthy, pungent, thick smoke.

When they had finished the three main rooms, Savana headed toward the stairs.

"Wait," Nick said quickly, "there is another room, a small bathroom under the stairs. It doesn't work so we never go in there."

"Good place for a spirit to hide." Savana said following him around the curved wall at the base of the stairs.

As she entered the small space, she had a vision of horrible abuse happening between a tiny girl and an old man. She turned away from it feeling sick to her stomach. This house held on to energy in a way she had not seen before.

They quickly filled the little room with smoke and then retreated to the main hall. Just as they started up the steps, they heard a loud slam! They looked at each other and Savana shrugged.

"That's why we are here." She said quietly, urging Nick forward.

As they got to the top of the stairs and peered down the hall, Nick could see that every door to every bedroom was shut. He knew they had been open the last time he was here. It would have been a memorable task to walk through and shut all the doors and he knew that he hadn't.

"They are making a feeble attempt to protect their space from the smoke." Savana said.

They started in the master bedroom and then the nursery. They moved across the hall from the nursery and into the small bedroom there.

"There is a secret passage that leads from the closet to the attic stairs." Nick said showing Savana the secret panel.

"Let's do the other bedrooms first and then we will do the passage before we go up to the attic."

They made their way through the rooms. Savana could feel the spirits retreat from them and she told Nick so.

"Good! Get outta my house you lousy bastards!" He shouted.

Just as the words left his mouth he got a punch right in the kidney. He whirled around but of course, no one was behind him. He looked at Savana whose eyes had gone wide.

"That is a very powerful presence." She said shakily. "Are you alright?" She asked Nick.

"Yeah, just a sucker punch! I thought they were retreating!" He said in an almost accusatory tone.

"They are. I don't know where that came from. It was just a burst of rage that filled the room for a split second before focusing like a laser beam right at you."

"Well, whatever we are doing must be working if we are getting them all riled up." Nick said.

"Yeah, maybe."

They finished the second floor by filling the only working bathroom with thick white smoke. They moved back the way they had come to enter the secret passage through the small bedroom's closet.

They had to crawl through the waist high opening like one would climb through a window. Once on the other side, Nick pulled the chain on the light fixture. The passage was narrow and short and the single bulb easily lit the entire length of the hall. Savana could stand up but Nick's 6' frame had to bend to walk through.

After carefully traversing the narrow passage and filling it with the sage smoke, they got to the other end. The door leading to the attic stairs was at head height. Luckily there were built in ladder steps making it easier to reach the latch.

Nick pulled on the mechanism but it wouldn't slide. It was a simple design, much like a sliding type that you would see on a back yard gate. Nick tried to wiggle it but it would not budge.

"Damn. The lock is stuck. It needs oil. I think I have some WD-40 under the kitchen sink. Do you want to come out of here while I get it?"

"Yeah, it's getting a bit smoky in here." Savana said, wishing she had not left her soda on the kitchen table.

They turned around and headed back down the 30-foot passage to the entrance at the closet. Nick had shut it so that the smoke would build up in the passage. Now he grabbed the handle on the inside of the small door and pulled. Nothing happened.

"What the hell?" Nick said out loud.

"Uh, oh." Savana said quietly.

"What? What is it?" Nick asked.

"I feel triumph, and murderous rage coming from both ends of the hall. They've trapped us on purpose!" She moved closer to Nick.

"Oh, hell no." Nick said with determination in his voice.

He grabbed the handle of the trap door and braced his foot against the wall. He pulled with all his might. The door didn't budge and Savana was starting to cough behind him.

"Let's put them out." He suggested.

"That's what they want. I don't see we have a choice though, the smoke is getting really thick."

They extinguished the sage bundles in the glasses of water they each carried. Nick was starting to feel a little pin prick of panic in his chest. He fought it, knowing he stood a better chance of getting out of here if he kept his wits about him.

Thinking that it would help dry them out and therefore enable them to be re-lit, he put the wet ends of the bundles in his flannel shirt pocket. A few seconds later, he felt a sharp sting on his chest, like a bee sting almost. It took another second to realize he was burning. The sage had rekindled!

He quickly, yanked the bundles from his pocket and dropped them on the floor. He stomped on them but each time he got one out, the other blazed back to life.

"They are trying to choke us!" Savana said, the panic in her voice all too evident.

"Damn it! I refuse to go out this way!" Nick began kicking at the door to the closet.

He couldn't get a good kick in, the door was too high and his balance too bad to get a lot of force at that angle.

"Nick its not working! Get low and try to call for help!"

Nick got to his knees and fumbled to get his phone out of his pocket. He swiped the screen and the phone lit up. Before he could even touch the phone icon, the phone beeped three times indicating battery drain and then blinked back off.

"It's drained!" He said to Savana.

"Damn it! They can do that. Zap energy out of just about anything electronic. I bet I would have the same problem if my phone were here instead of in my purse in my car."

"Fuck!" Nick shouted.

The sage continued to burn and the smoke was getting so thick that breathing was becoming harder. Nick was fully prepared to panic when Savana held up her hand.

"Wait! I feel something happening! Someone is here!"

"Someone or something?" Nick asked.

"A soul. I can feel her. She is fighting with the energy that is keeping the doors shut!"

"Who is she?" Nick feared for a moment that something had happened to Julianne.

"It's a woman, she died living here many years ago, she is trapped here and is tired of watching this house bring misery and evil to the people who live here. That's all I can get."

Her sentence was punctuated by an enormous sound. It was not quite a scream or howl, not really a growl but something guttural and primitive. Both Nick and Savana crawled back away from the sound. Just when he thought he couldn't stand it another second, the hatch at the bedroom closet flew off its hinges and shot over the tops of their heads.

The smoke began rolling out of the small opening and the room was instantly quiet. They did not hesitate to climb out of the small space. Savana began coughing and sat down on the floor.

"Well, that did not go as planned." Nick stated the obvious.

"No... and I don't think we should go any further.... There is a serious... energy ...building in the attic and I don't think sage is going to be an adequate defense." She said between coughs.

"What do you think is going to happen?" Nick asked, coughing a bit himself.

"I honestly don't know but I don't think you are dealing with just lost souls here."

"What do you think we are dealing with?"

"The house. It has energy of its own. I have never felt anything like it. I think it's the house that is making people sick."

"How is that possible?" Nick asked, running his hand through his hair. He couldn't wrap his brain around it.

"Frankly, I don't know."

Chapter Twenty-Seven

After Savana's Toyota pulled out of the drive, Nick jumped in to his own car and drove straight to the hospital. He had his laptop and the thumb drive that Jordan Hawkes had given him. It was time to tell Julianne the truth. She needed to know that it was not safe to return to that house.

He wasn't sure of the policy on electronics in the hospital but he could not wait for her to be released. They needed to decide together what they were going to do. He just hoped the evidence would convince her to cut their losses and move back to New York. He didn't even want to try to sell the house. It could sit there empty for eternity as far as he was concerned.

He tucked the lab top into a book bag and put some clothes on top of it. Hopefully they would just assume he was bringing fresh items to his wife. The flash drive he tucked into his front pants pocket. With a deep breath and weak resolve, he headed in through the front doors.

The ladies at the front desk recognized him from his many visits over the past week. They smiled and waived and no one asked about the bag. He adjusted the strap over his shoulder and walked toward his wife's room.

His heart about exploded out of his chest when hospital security strolled around the corner and came straight at him. He tried not to show his guilty conscience but he did feel his step falter slightly. When the guard was within a few feet, Nick forced himself to meet his eyes and nod hello. The guard gave him a quick tight smile and kept walking.

Nick thought his knees would buckle with relief when he reached Julianne's room. He looked quickly up and down the hall before stepping inside and shutting the door. Julianne looked up from her magazine and smiled.

He hated the fact that he was about to wipe that smile away. He remembered the happiness they had shared at the time they decided to buy the house. He shook his head; it seemed a lifetime ago. He felt stupid remembering that he had kept the rumors about ghosts from his wife. He did not tell her about the death and sickness that had invaded every family that had lived there.

"What is it Nick?" Julianne asked with some alarm.

He felt the tears sting the back of his eyes as he lowered himself into the chair next to her bed.

"The girls?" She could barely get the words out around the fear in her chest.

"No! The girls are fine; in fact they're great. It's not anything to do with them. Well... not directly anyway." He was stumbling over his words unsure how to begin.

"I need to tell you something. I have kept things from you and now I need to tell you."

"Nick, you're scaring me!"

"I know, I know and I am sorry, but Jules we need to be afraid."

He began at the beginning and told his wife about the rumors and history and how he had kept it from her because he was afraid she would pass up a chance at a dream home because of superstition.

He told her about Savana doing a reading on the house and the things she had seen. He told her about the rape and murder that took place in their kitchen all those years ago. He told her how the ghost of that serving woman though *he* was the man responsible."

"Wait... your telling me that a woman was killed in our kitchen in 18-whatever, and she is blaming you? That doesn't make any sense."

"It would appear that she is trapped in her grief and anger and she is confused by an energy in the house. She has attacked more than one of the previous owners."

"This is a lot Nick, I don't understand why you are telling me now, what has happened?"

Nick rose from the chair and peaked into the hall, checking for nurses or security. The hall was blessedly empty. He shut the door and pulled the blinds on the window down and twisted them shut.

"I have something to show you." Nick pulled flash drive out of his pocket and held it out for her to see.

"What is that?" She asked, slightly annoyed.

Nick pulled the laptop out of the bag and set it on her tray table. He booted it up and was glad to see that there was plenty of battery life. He plugged the flash drive into the USB port.

He explained to Julianne about the PRISM team and what they do. He told her about the personal experiences they had in the house. He clicked on the videos and audio files one by one, watching his wife's face tighten more and more with each one.

When he got to the end, he closed the laptop and looked at his wife. He could see a range of emotion play across her features. Tears welled up and spilled over the brim of her lower lids. His heart broke for her.

"So, let me get this straight," she said in an even almost cold tone. "The house is responsible for my heart condition?"

"It's possible. Everyone who has owned that house has become ill." Nick said sliding his hands down his face. He felt like he was trying to wipe the truth away.

"Listen, Jules, we are going to be okay. We don't even need to sell the house. We will just pack up everything and head back to New York."

"The house, or maybe the ghosts that are in it, are the reason my babies were born too early?" He could see her trying to wrap her mind around it.

"I'm so sorry Jules. I should have told you the truth before we bought the house. If you had wanted to walk away, we…"

"STOP IT!" She nearly screamed at him.

He looked up startled and met his wife's eyes. He had never seen the look in her eyes before.

"Jules…"

"No! We are not going to blame each other or ourselves." She said each word carefully and clearly.

The relief was too much for him. He was so worried she would hold him responsible. He let the tears slide gratefully down his cheeks.

"No we aren't going to do that either." She said reaching up to wipe the tears from his cheeks.

"What do you want to do?" Nick asked.

"There is only one thing to do." She said with ferocity in her voice.

She looked him straight in the eye and said, "Burn it."

Chapter Twenty-Eight

Nick felt like everyone knew what he was doing. He was trying very hard to be inconspicuous. He lounged back against the car in a false posture of patience. Inside he was urging the gas pump to hurry up and fill the fourth, five-gallon can in his trunk.

He had stopped at four different gas stations to fill up each can. He didn't want anyone to see how much gasoline he was purchasing and start asking questions. Questions he could not possibly answer.

If he admitted to anyone that he was planning to burn down his house because it was trying to kill people, he would be locked up in the mental ward at the hospital. It sounded ridiculous, even in his head. Even after all he had seen. So, he went cloak and dagger to get what he needed.

He found himself wondering what was going to happen. Would the house burn quickly? Would it burn quietly? He wondered if it would let loose its primitive growl while it was dying in the blaze. Just remembering the sound they had heard while in the secret passage was enough to make him shudder.

He filled the last can to the brim and wound the cap tightly back on. He didn't want to spill it in the car. He wanted every last drop to fall in the house. He wondered briefly if it was against the law to burn ones own home down. He didn't plan on making an insurance claim. What could they do? Reckless Endangerment maybe. He would deal with that when the time came.

He shut the rear door on the neat row of large gas cans. *It'll be enough,* he told himself. He really had no idea how much gas it would take to burn down such a large house. He wanted to leave no part of it standing. Nowhere for the evil to remain hidden, while biding its time until another unsuspecting family drove up.

"Over my dead body." He said aloud as he leaned into the seat of his Jeep. He hoped it wouldn't come to that.

The U-Haul he had picked up that morning was parked in the driveway. He planned to load as much as he could by himself. It meant losing the larger pieces of furniture but he would be able to get the keepsakes and mementos from their life; things that are not easily replaced.

As he pulled along side the 14' truck, his skin began to crawl. *What if it knows?* He shook the thought off, knowing if he continued to think along those lines, he would chicken out. He couldn't fail Julianne. Not this time. It was just too important.

He turned the Jeep around and backed into the carport. With the sun beginning to set the shadows would help conceal his activity. Plus the U Haul was parked by design, at an angle that blocked the view from most of the street.

He sat in the Jeep, revisiting his plan. First, he would load the truck, then carry all four of the gas cans in before starting to pour. His heart skipped a little beat at the thought of pouring the flammable liquid throughout the house. It occurred to him that if the house or the spirits within knew what the sage sticks were for, surely they would understand what he was doing with the gas. *Please God be with me on this quest.*

When he felt certain he knew every step he would take once inside, he stepped out of the Jeep. He opened the door from the carport to the kitchen. Immediately the hair on his arms and neck stood up. He wasn't sure if he was just creeped out by everything that had happened here, or if his instincts were trying to tell him something.

Either way, he knew what he had to do. He could not let this house ruin another family. It had to be burned beyond repair. He tried not to think about it while he was inside. He didn't know if the house could read his thoughts.

"Jesus, I have gone fucking nuts." He said aloud. "Okay, house. You win!" He shouted into the empty air.

"We are leaving. I am just going to pack some things first and then I will go!" Hopefully that would keep the activity to a minimum while he loaded the truck.

Luckily, they had not unpacked a lot of the boxes. They had wanted to paint and sand floors before scattering too many belongings around the rooms. So the first item on his agenda was to get those boxes out. Then he would take furniture, gradually increasing in size until he came to a point he could lift nothing further.

He moved quickly from room to room taking the most important boxes first. He could feel the house watching him. The extra adrenaline and fear helped keep him moving at a quickened pace. It took less time than he thought it would and with less activity than he anticipated.

The sun had just dipped below the horizon as he slammed the door on the U-Haul shut. He would wait the few minutes, until complete darkness, before he carried the gas inside. He went into the kitchen to grab a cold beer out of the refrigerator. He would leave the rest of the food behind. He wasn't entirely clear on their travel plans after the fire.

As he sat on the front stoop, he noticed that the woman he had seen before was back on her porch. Again, her hand fiddled nervously at her neck. She was staring right at him. He lifted his bottle as way of greeting. It was apparently enough acknowledgment to make her mind up about something. She started down her drive in his direction.

Nick stood and stretched before sauntering across the gravel drive to meet the woman. Just as she reached the end of the driveway, she stopped. She looked meaningfully at Nick so he quickened his pace to meet her where she was.

"Hello." Nick said trying hard to make his voice sound friendly.

"Hello. Mr. Sullivan right?"

Nick was surprised; he had never talked to any of his neighbors and didn't have a clue as to what this woman's name was.

"Yes but please call me Nick." He held out his hand to shake. "I'm sorry, you are...?"

"Phyllis. Phyllis Walker"

"Pleasure. Sorry we haven't been around to introduce ourselves." He said wondering what Phyllis wanted to say.

"No one is going to come to you either. But it looks like the point is moot. You're moving out?" She inclined her head toward the moving truck.

"Yeah, turns out we miss New York so..."

"I've lived on this street for forty years. I know about the house Mr. Sullivan."

"What do you know?" He asked not wanting to be the first to say it.

"It's evil and it's haunted." She said matter-of-factly.

She looked up at the attic window before she looked Nick square in the eye. "It destroys people. It abuses people like a drunk beats his wife."

"I don't understand your meaning." Nick said feeling a bit confused.

"Let me ask you this Mr. Sullivan."

"Nick." He repeated.

"Okay, Nick. Do you know when the most dangerous time for an abused woman is?"

"No. I don't" He said not sure what she was getting at.

"When she tries to leave." Phyllis looked at the U-Haul and back at the house.

"Just be careful Mr. Sullivan, Nick. You made the right choice when you decided to leave but you also made a dangerous one." With that, she turned and crossed the street to her own home without looking back.

He wondered if she somehow knew what he was planning to do.

Chapter Twenty-Nine

Nick stood in the driveway looking at the house. The shadows were finally fading to pure black. He took the final swig of his beer and set the bottle on the back bumper of the U-Haul. He squared his shoulders and marched into the carport. He popped the back of the Jeep open and grabbed two of the five-gallon cans.

It was a struggle to get them out and carry both to the house but he didn't want to make four trips. He used his foot to push the door open wide and looked into the darkness of the kitchen. He could feel his pulse begin to race. A shallow film of perspiration formed on his forehead. Despite having just finished a beer, his mouth was incredibly dry.

He entered the darkness and set the first can of gas down by the door. The second, he carried to the back staircase. He looked up the steps but could barely see beyond the bottom two. He didn't dare turn on the light. He couldn't afford to have a neighbor see him through the windows as he poured the gas.

He pulled his phone out of his pocket and turned on the flashlight feature. The light was fairly bright but he didn't think it was bright enough to give him away. It was at least less conspicuous that the overhead lighting.

Aiming the light at the stairs, he climbed to the top. He left the heavy jug there and quickly retreated back down the steps. He crossed the kitchen and stepped through the door. As he cleared the steps, the door slammed shut behind him.

It knows. He felt himself begin to shake in earnest. He took a deep breath to steady his nerves and picked up the two remaining gas cans from the Jeep.

That's right. This ends tonight. He thought towards the house. He refused to deviate from his plan. It could slam all the doors it wanted. He would just open them back up. The kitchen door opened surprisingly easy. He expected there to be some resistance.

He hurried through the kitchen, down the great hall and to the grand staircase. He set one of the gas cans at the bottom and carried the last one up the stairs. He trotted back down and picked up the can he left at the bottom and pulled the cap off. The somewhat pleasant smell of the gas permeated the hall. He tilted the can and began to pour.

He poured a steady stream from the kitchen door, through the dining room and across the hall to the library. He hesitated as he looked at all the books. He was tempted for a moment to grab a few stacks and run them out to the car before he lit the fire but then he spotted the books on the floor.

He touched his newly healed lip as he remembered how they flew off the shelf. He hesitated no longer. He even splashed a few rows of books, just for good measure. He trailed the gas out of the library through to the living room and back around to the main stairs. He had just enough gas left to douse each of the stairs on his way up to the second floor.

As he reached the top of the stairs, he was momentarily blinded as every light in the house blazed to life. He blinked a few times and looked at the large window on the landing. *It want's me to be seen!*

Deciding that he didn't care, he picked up the second can of gas. He popped off the cap and dribbled toward the master bedroom, splashing the outer door to the nursery as he went. The resistance he expected from the kitchen door met with him instead at the bedroom. He couldn't get the knob to turn.

His memory took him back to when he was locked out and Julianne was locked in, having an episode with her heart. The pictures that played out in his mind stoked his rage. He lifted his foot and gave the door a powerful kick. The door splintered and sailed open with a bang against the wall.

As he stepped through the threshold he heard a deep, horrible growl. It was guttural and primal, just as he remembered it from the secret passage. Despite his resolve, his fear bubbled up in his throat.

"Fuck you!" He screamed.

He began tossing the gas around the room and telling the house about its fate.

"That's right you're gonna burn! Every floor board, every window sill, every plaster wall is going to be reduced to ASHES!"

He pushed open the door to the nursery and started to walk through. He was caught by surprise when the door flew back at him and slammed into his body, the brunt of which hit his shoulder. He cursed but he kept moving. He poured his trail out the nursery and into the bedroom across the hall. The closet was open and he could see into the passage through the broken secret door. He didn't want to go in there again, even with the door broken. So he stood at the entrance and flung streams of gas as far into the hall as he could.

He emptied the second gas can as he moved down the hall past the three other bedrooms. He shook puddles of gas into each one. When he reached the room closest to the bathroom, he spied the toy box in the closet. He doused it quickly and got out of the room before the box decided to roll after him.

As he reached the top of the back stairs he tossed the empty can aside and picked up the third full can. He braced himself, knowing he had to be sure it all burned. He wanted to run, light what was already poured and just go. But he didn't. Instead, he picked up the can and headed to the attic.

He opened the door and was immediately shoved backwards into the stair well. He was forced to drop the gas can to grab the railing and keep from tumbling head over heals to the bottom. The gas can fell down a couple of stairs and started to spill its contents.

He grabbed at it quickly and threw it through the open doorway into the middle of the attic floor. He watched as the puddle began to spread out from beneath it. It would have to do. He just couldn't bring himself to go inside. He carefully but quickly retreated down the stairs.

He didn't linger upstairs either. He headed straight down the back stairs to the final can of gasoline sitting in the kitchen.

Only it wasn't where he left it. He scanned the room but couldn't see where the large red plastic can was sitting. His frustration began to mount. He hadn't gotten any gas in the kitchen. He needed to be able to light the gas from the door so he could get out as soon as the blaze was lit. He had planned to use the gas to create a trail from the stairs to the kitchen door.

He looked quickly in each of the cupboards that would be big enough to hold the 4'x3' can. He checked the pantry and the rooms on the bottom floor. He didn't find it anywhere.

"Fuck!" He screamed again

"You think that will stop me?" He asked the house. "Don't count on it!"

In response, the lights went out and he once again felt a jolt that put him on his knees. This one was more powerful than the one he had gotten the night he saw the blue light. It took him a few seconds to catch his breath. He pulled his cell phone back out of his pocket and shined the light on his side.

There were four jagged red marks on his flesh. Not like a claw mark, not like what he had seen in the picture of Maggie's back. This looked more like a small hot brand had been placed against his skin. The four jagged lines had some symmetry to them, like a symbol. He let his shirt drop; at least it wasn't bleeding.

He also wasn't deterred. He did however feel a new sense of urgency and decided to abandon his search for the last gas can and just light what was already poured. He could light the trail at the top of the stairs. It would ignite the upstairs hall first; giving him time to race down the stairs and out the carport door before the downstairs was completely engulfed.

He took the back stairs two at a time on the way up. He flashed his light around until he found the where the wet trail had soaked into the carpet. Straightening his spine, he pulled a book of matches from his pocket. He struck the first one and it immediately went out. He struck a second one and the same thing happened.

Is it really blowing the matches out? If he weren't so frightened, it would have struck him as funny. Instead it frustrated him immensely. *What do I do now?*

He bent down close to the gas spill and cupped his hand and tried again. This time the fumes from the gas caught before he could get his face away. He felt the singe of his eyelashes and brows. He didn't care. The fire was lit! The flames were dancing ghostly down the haul. The fumes and fixtures alternately were bursting into flames. It made it look as though the fire was dancing down the hall. Very quickly.

He turned and headed back to the stairs. He took two steps down when his feet were kicked out from underneath him. He fell hard onto his back, hearing a crack that was most likely a disc shattering in his spine. He groaned and tried to suck in a lung full of air. His body would not cooperate. What he did manage to suck in tasted of gas and burned wood. The taste sent a wave of fear pulsing through his body.

He grabbed the railing and yanked himself into a sitting position. The pain in his back screamed in protest. He began to cough. The upper floor was in complete blaze and the smoke was filling the stairs. He used the railing and limped his way down the stairs.

He had taken too long. The fire had already followed the trail of gas down the stairs and through the hall. The old wooden kitchen door went up like a match. He had to get close to it to get out through the carport door. He pulled his shirt up over his nose and mouth and ran to the door. The locks were all engaged! He had left them open for a quick escape.

The smoke from the door was pouring into the kitchen and had already filled the top half of the room with smoke. He could smell the rancid smell of burning plastic and carpet. It was starting to choke him.

He dropped to his knees and tried to unlock the door but the locks would not turn! He ran quickly to the door that led to the back porch and tried to open it as well. It too was locked tight.

I can't die in here! Julianne needs me! I can't leave her alone to raise our daughters! My daughter's need me! I have to get out!

He looked around at the burning room. There was no other way out. His vision started to blur. He blinked away the hot tears that were forming in response to the thick smoke. It didn't help to clear his vision and he was feeling a bit lightheaded. He remembered from school that it took less than 60-seconds to become disoriented from smoke inhalation during a fire. He was running out of time!

He was starting to forget what he was doing, his thoughts were becoming muddled. He looked around the room and darkness started to form at the edges of his vision. *I am not going to make it!*

Just then, a large crash came from the back of the kitchen. A large chunk of concrete skidded across the floor surrounded by pieces of stained glass. The fire roared higher with a new influx of oxygen.

"Mr. Sullivan! Mr. Sullivan can you hear me?" It was Phyllis from across the street!

"Yes. Here." He said, his voice hoarse and not very loud compared to the roaring of the fire.

"Can you get to the window Mr. Sullivan?"

Nick began to crawl toward the sound of his neighbor's voice. The beam of a flashlight caught him in the eyes.

"There!" He heard Phyllis shout. It was the last thing he would remember about the fire. His lungs seized and his vision faded to black.

Chapter Thirty

When Nick opened his eyes, he was laying in the grass. A paramedic was talking to him but he was too confused to understand what was being said. He put his hand to his face and found an oxygen mask covering the lower half. The paramedic asked him a question again.

"Can you hear me Nick? Do you understand my words?" He was pulling open Nick's eyelids and flashing a pin light back and forth over his pupils.

Nick tried to answer but when he opened his mouth a violent spasm of coughing shook his entire body.

"Okay, okay easy does it. Just nod if you can hear me."

Nick nodded as the cough subsided. He closed his eyes and tried hard to clear the fog from his brain. He was starting to remember what was going on. He looked over the shoulder of the medic and could see the house totally encompassed in flames. The fire department was on scene shooting large trunks of jetting water at the blaze.

"Let it burn." He whispered and closed his eyes again.

"Okay he's responsive! Let's get em in the bus!" He said loudly and the other paramedic joined him at Nick's side.

"You almost burned up from the look of things. It's a good thing your neighbor caught sight of the blaze before you were cooked.

Though you have some pretty serious burns on your arms and legs." The first paramedic went on as they lifted Nick on to the gurney and then lifted the gurney into the ambulance.

Waves of pain were starting to course through his body. He didn't remember getting burned but it must have been when he tried to get out the carport door. He had gotten too close to the interior kitchen door.

He moaned as the shock began to wear off and his legs started to feel like they were still on fire. Tears once again rolled down his cheek. *I hadn't cried since fifth grade, until I came to Missouri. Maybe they got it right when the locals called it Misery.*

"He we go, I am going to give you a shot of morphine Mr. Sullivan, it will help with the pain."

It only took seconds for the morphine to work its way into his bloodstream. The pain began to ebb and mercifully he slept.

Epilogue

Nick sat watching Julianne play with the twins, Jackie and Serena, who were trying to use Atlas and Asia to pull themselves upright. They were about to turn one year old and were not showing any signs of being behind the learning curve as preemies so often did. It was a warm day for a February in New York and they took the opportunity to get out and go to the park.

He looked back down at the two envelopes he held in his hand. He had plucked them from the growing pile of mail by the apartment door on the way out. The first had arrived a week ago but he couldn't bring himself to open it. He stared at the Buchanan County seal on the corner of the envelope. It was from the fire investigator. The words inside would seal his fate and he wasn't really ready to face up to it just yet. As long as he didn't look, there was still the opportunity for the cause of the fire to be undetermined. It had burned so completely, there wasn't much left to examine.

He absent-mindedly stroked the scar on his leg through his jeans as he looked at the second envelope he held. This one had arrived earlier that day. It was also from St. Joseph but not from any official. This one was from Phyllis. He decided to open this one first.

Dear Nick and Julianne,

I hope this letter finds you well. I was amazed to learn of the verdict in your case. It seems as though God was looking out for you this time around. Congratulations.

I wanted to write a brief note to tell you that a developer has started making noises about buying your land. So far, no one has given him your contact information but I have enclosed his business card if you would like to get in touch with him.

I hope you don't sell that land Nick. The energy still lingers. You can feel it if you take just one step onto the lot. Maybe you could turn the lot into a garden? Perhaps a memorial? Something that would not require a permanent structure to be built. Just a thought. Anyway, hope your winter is going well and I wish you the best of luck in the future. May all of God's blessings be yours.

Sincerely,

Phyllis Walker

Nick read the letter again. He thought for a moment about Phyllis' request, a park or monument or memorial. All good suggestions but all of them would tie him and his family to that God-awful property for life. He glanced up at his family and saw that Julianne was watching him. She had such a haunted look in her eyes.

He quickly opened the other letter and scanned the words. He finally found it.

Cause of fire: Undetermined.

Hey looked up and caught Julianne's curious gaze. He smiled briefly at her and fingered the business card Phyllis had sent him. After several moments of consideration he pulled out his phone and dialed.

"Ron Hux." A man answered on the second ring.

'Yeah, Mr. Hux my name is Nick Sullivan. I have been informed that you want to buy my land at 11th and Messanie. Yeah, I would like to hear your offer."

Phyllis Walker would just have to forgive him.